Agustín Fernández Paz

NOTHING REALLY MATTERS
IN LIFE MORE THAN LOVE

Published in 2018 by
SMALL STATIONS PRESS
20 Dimitar Manov Street, 1408 Sofia, Bulgaria
You can order books and contact the publisher at
www.smallstations.com

This book was first published in the Galician language as *O único que queda é o amor* by Edicións Xerais de Galicia (Vigo, 2007). A list of our fiction titles can be found at www.smallstations.com/fiction. More information about the author can be found at www.agustinfernandezpaz.gal. More information about the illustrator can be found at www.pabloauladell.com

The story "This Strange Lucidity" previously appeared in the anthology *Best European Fiction 2012*, edited by Aleksandar Hemon and published by Dalkey Archive Press in 2011. There are quotations in this book from: *2046*, film directed and written by Wong Kar-wai; Franz Kafka, *The Penal Colony: Stories and Short Pieces*, tr. Willa and Edwin Muir (Schocken Books, 1948); *Hearts in Atlantis*, film directed by Scott Hicks, written by William Goldman and based on the book by Stephen King; Jacob and Wilhelm Grimm, *Grimm's Fairy Tales*, tr. Lucy Crane (Hurst & Co., 1882); José Ángel Valente, *Landscape with Yellow Birds*, tr. Thomas Christensen (Archipelago Books, 2013); Manuel Rivas, *Vermeer's Milkmaid and Other Stories*, tr. Jonathan Dunne (Vintage, 2003); Orhan Pamuk, *Snow*, tr. Maureen Freely (Vintage, 2005); Pablo Neruda, *Selected Poems: A Bilingual Edition*, ed. Nathaniel Tarn, tr. Anthony Kerrigan, W. S. Merwin, Alastair Reid and Nathaniel Tarn (Houghton Mifflin/Seymour Lawrence, 1990); Paul Auster, *Moon Palace* (Penguin Books, 1990); Paul Auster, *Oracle Night: A Novel* (Picador, 2009); Paul Éluard, "The Curve of Your Eyes," tr. A. S. Kline (http://poetsofmodernity.xyz/POMBR/French/Eluard.htm); W. B. Yeats, *The Wind among the Reeds* (J. Lane, The Bodley Head, 1899); *Wings of Desire*, film directed by Wim Wenders and written by Wim Wenders, Peter Handke and Richard Reitinger

This work received a grant from the General Secretariat of Culture of the Ministry of Culture, Education and University Planning of the Xunta de Galicia in the call for translation grants of the year 2017

Esta obra recibiu unha axuda da Secretaría Xeral de Cultura da Consellería de Cultura, Educación e Ordenación Universitaria da Xunta de Galicia na convocatoria de axudas para a tradución do ano 2017

ISBN 978-954-384-086-1

Agustín Fernández Paz

Nothing Really Matters in Life More Than Love

WINNER
OF THE
SPANISH NATIONAL
BOOK AWARD FOR
YOUNG PEOPLE'S
LITERATURE

Illustrated by Pablo Auladell
Translated from Galician by Jonathan Dunne

SMALL
STATIONS
PRESS

CONTENTS

When I see so many people around me leading such stupid lives and then vanishing without a trace, an anger runs through me because I know then nothing really matters in life more than love.

Orhan Pamuk, *Snow* (tr. Maureen Freely)

A Radiant Silence

All memories are traces of tears.

Wong Kar-wai, 2046

A t the end of the meeting held every morning by the bank's board of directors, Sara retreated to her office and slumped in a chair opposite the large tinted window. From up here she could contemplate the lower part of the city, which sloped gently down to the flat area of the port, with fewer boats than usual. Beyond that was the vast sea, a sea she avoided looking at on days like this, perhaps so as not to be swept away by the wave of nostalgia for open spaces that sometimes overwhelmed her.

At such moments, she couldn't stop the obsessions that recently crowded her mind. She knew everyone considered her professional situation excellent, no one had got so far being so young. The merit was even greater because she was a woman, she should feel proud of her achievements. But she wasn't, though this was a secret she kept to herself. Only she knew all those operations she carried out so efficiently had ceased to interest her months before, she was bored by the endless sessions analyzing movements in the market or new investment plans. Her salary was high, that was true, she could buy anything that took her fancy. Except for time, she thought bitterly, time that seemed to take wing as if the hours were a flock of migratory birds heading south. She spent many hours shut up in her crystal tower, as required to in the daytime, but also in the evening, a routine she hadn't minded until something inside her had changed and she'd realized life, real life, was flowing relentlessly by on the other side of the glass walls. It was then she remembered a children's story her father always told her, "Rapunzel," a story that both fascinated and disturbed her when she was little. The image of that unfortunate girl shut away forever in a tower with no doors or stairs, letting the hours go by while the hair that would eventually save her grew and grew, seemed an accurate metaphor for her and the life she was leading.

She also lived alone, in a duplex facing the sea. The decoration was minimal. Books, CDs and films took up most of the space, while pictures by young painters covered the walls. Painting, music, books, films... these passions had grown with her from her teens. She sometimes liked to fantasize about how her life would have been, had she dedicated herself professionally to one of them. But family pressure, together with her own ambition, had told in the end and she'd chosen the career with the greatest social prestige. It was only here, in the intimate space she'd created, where she managed to feel comfortable, though, like Rapunzel stuck in her tower, she felt an ever stronger desire to share her life with someone who had similar tastes and would free her from the torment of her days, someone she was quite sure she would never meet in the circles she currently moved in.

She looked down and gazed at the pavement opposite. The works were almost finished, the inauguration was set for the following Saturday. How brave daring to open a bookshop in the current climate! She hadn't been at all surprised when the fabric shop that had been there before had closed, an old shop she'd remembered as a child, whose chances of survival had been zero. When it had closed, three or four months earlier, she'd thought they would open another of the many businesses filling that central zone: an estate agent's, a shop for electrical goods, a boutique… She'd been taken aback when she saw the sign announcing the forthcoming opening of a bookshop. There wasn't one in that area, speculative greed had pushed them all out to the margins. A further consequence of the unwritten laws governing the world they lived in, where priority was given to short-term profit. It wasn't going to be easy to keep going in such a hostile environment.

The vision of the bookshop went some way to soothing Sara's unease. When it opened, she would have the perfect excuse to avoid the half hour of coffee she shared with the other directors, almost all of whom were men, when all they did was talk about the same topics as in their work meetings or, worse still, about male themes that held no interest for her. All strangers, like the inhabitants of another planet, thought Sara from time to time. Though it might be said, as in *I Am Legend*, that disturbing book by Richard Matheson, she was the stranger, the only resident alien.

Sara didn't go there the day of the inauguration, but the following Monday she took her coffee break early and, instead of heading for the café where she normally met her colleagues from the bank, she crossed the street and entered the bookshop. She was surprised by the amount of space and the taste with which everything had been arranged. She was even more surprised to find a small cafeteria at the back of the shop, with a modest counter and four tables in an area limited by shelves that, like the radii of an imaginary circle, seemed to converge in one of the corners. It was a magnificent idea, which Sara had seen in several cities she'd visited, but no one had dared to set up in her own. It was also an ideal solution for her. She could have her morning coffee there every day and, at the same time, lose herself among all the volumes on display on the shelves and tables.

The shop seemed to have been prepared so that customers could feel safe in the knowledge that no one would disturb them. There were only two people in charge: the man who looked after the till and checked the shelves, arranging books and responding to customers' queries, and a slightly older woman who ran the cafeteria and, as Sara soon found out, also worked the computer that had all the books catalogued on it.

Sara sat down at one of the tables and ordered a cup of coffee and some toast. She felt extraordinarily peaceful that morning, observing everything going on around her. There weren't many customers, six or seven people wandering down the aisles, perhaps because it was a Monday. Sara walked down the aisles as well, feeling excited by what she discovered. It was obvious the shop had been designed to cover needs others didn't see to. All the bestsellers were on the tables, those even the smallest bookshop couldn't go without, but she also found minority collections that were missing in others.

She was drawn most of all to the section devoted to poetry, a large shelf that took up most of the far wall, covered in titles and authors she viewed with emotion. She'd always liked poetry, even though it was a facet of her life she'd never shared during her time at university, and certainly not in any of the jobs she'd had. "Rapunzel in her loneliness tried to pass away the time with sweet songs." This is what poetry was for her, the song that helped her to feel alive, a vice or secret passion that kept her from falling into despair.

That day, she left the shop with two books, an edition of the letters Kafka wrote to Milena Jesenská, a volume she thought was out of print, and *Moment*, a recent work by Wisława Szymborska, the Polish writer who'd impressed her greatly when she'd read *View with a Grain of Sand*, one of the few books she always kept close at hand since it possessed the virtue, whatever page she opened to, of filling her with the joy of life, such was its sense of optimism. She'd have liked to take a few more, there were many titles she was interested in, but her rational side had quickly imposed itself: if she was going to visit that shop every day, the normal thing would be to buy a single book each time and so prolong the pleasure of making a selection.

The first few days, out of curiosity or perhaps just to please her, some colleagues from the bank went with her. But they soon grew tired of the novelty and returned to the huddle of the group. For Sara, her trips to the bookshop turned into a happy routine. She was on familiar terms with the man at the till by now, and the woman in the cafeteria always prepared her coffee and toast as soon as she saw her come in. Almost every day, she spent most of her time immersed in the poetry section, busy selecting the title she would buy that morning. Back in her office, she would always find the time to forget her work and, sitting opposite the window, be carried along by the words, so full of life, which, even just for a few moments, made her forget the tall tower she also felt trapped in.

One morning, on heading for the poetry section as normal after drinking her coffee, Sara noticed something strange. Sticking out between two books in a way that made it difficult to miss was a small, blue piece of card. She took it, intrigued. The card was long and, on one of its sides, had a few handwritten verses:

Your body can
fill my life,
just as your laughter
can drive away the dark wall
of sadness.

A single word from you breaks
blind solitude to bits.

She was overcome with emotion on reading these verses, rarely had she felt so much intensity in so few words, distilled in them as they say matter is in the nucleus of some stars. She read them over and over again, shaken to the core, while shooting glances this way and that to see if anyone had noticed her embarrassment. But nobody seemed to be paying attention to her or to the card trembling in her hands.

When she turned it over, she saw the title of a book and the name of its author were written on the other side. Without a doubt, this had to be the volume the verses had been taken from. She quickly searched on the shelf for the section corresponding to the letter V and soon found the book she was looking for: *Point Zero* by José Ángel Valente. She urgently flicked through it until finding the page indicated in brackets at the end of the verses. There was the whole poem, "Be My Limit," more powerful and stirring than the first verses promised, a delicate combination of passion and beauty that grew in intensity until it burst in the stunning final verses, which, once read, could never be forgotten.

Sara clutched the book to her chest, perhaps to muffle the sudden loud thumping of her heart. Before leaving, she checked the shelf to see if there were any other pieces of card; it may have been a new selling technique, a very effective one at that. But no, there were no more cards on this shelf or any of the others she perused on her way to the till. She paid for the book without hearing the kind words the man addressed to her and left the shop with the impression that, while her surroundings hadn't changed, there was something different in the air that enabled her to see everything with new eyes.

Back in her office, she opened the book and examined the card more carefully. There were the verses that had moved her so much, written in fine handwriting, the letters drawn with all the delicacy of a Chinese ideogram. Sara's surprise was boundless when, on looking closer, she found her name in one of the corners on the back, written with pencil in tiny letters, so tiny she hadn't noticed them at first glance. This card had been addressed to her, someone had placed it there for her to find!

After a few moments' confusion, Sara tried to disentangle the threads of this mystery. It had to be someone who knew her, who was familiar with her habits, her movements in the bookshop. Who could it be? Other people, like her, visited the shop almost daily, people with whom she felt a certain complicity, though they'd never exchanged a word. Could it be the man who regularly sat at a table next to hers? She'd noticed him more than once, he was very handsome, impossible not to admire his silver hair and grey-blue eyes so full of life, in which Sara detected a hint of sadness. Of course it could also be the young man who always sat on a stool at the counter. He dressed informally and, for reading, used small rimless glasses that made him highly attractive in Sara's eyes. She'd caught him looking at her on occasion, they'd even exchanged a fleeting smile. There were other men who came into the shop at the same time, but these two were the only regulars. In the absence of further proof, Sara concluded, or rather wished, it was one of these strangers who had sent her the card.

The following morning, on entering the bookshop, Sara headed straight for the shelf at the back. Since the previous day, a new joy had been struggling to blossom inside her despite the fact she knew it was a ridiculous sensation sustained only by a few weak threads. But as soon as she reached the books, she forgot all her misgivings and her eyes were drawn like a magnet to the far right, where there was a new card, this time pale pink in colour. It also had a few verses, written in the same painstaking handwriting as the last time:

If only you would touch my heart,
if only you would put your lips to my heart,
your delicate mouth, your teeth,
if you would place your tongue like a red arrow
where my crumbling heart is beating...

Although she thought she'd heard or read them before, these simple verses similarly aroused Sara's feelings; whoever selected them knew her tastes very well. The book's title and author were written on the other side, though the first thing she glanced at were the tiny, faint letters of her name, which again appeared in one of the corners. Holding the card, she turned towards the small cafeteria. Her eyes met those of the young man, who immediately blushed and looked away, no doubt because she had caught him staring. Meanwhile, the man with the grey-blue eyes continued reading the newspaper, oblivious to what was going on around him.

She searched in confusion for the book, and soon found it: Pablo Neruda's *Selected Poems*. She went straight to the page indicated on the card, though she was already sure the whole poem would be much more forceful and emotional than the verses at the start. She was right, it was. Sara's legs shook as she succumbed to the wealth of images that seemed intended to sweep through her heart like a gale. How could she have lived so many years without knowing this poem? And no doubt, inside the book, there would be other poems just as memorable, as there had been in the first book. A feast, a flood of words and emotions that would help melt the frozen windows of her claustrophobic tower.

She took the book and headed for the till. Halfway there, she stopped dead in her tracks. Next to one of the tables with new publications, she'd spotted a colleague from the bank, possibly the only one who still hankered after something other than the accumulation of wealth as his only objective. What if he was the one who had been sending her these messages? He may have felt obliged to hide his sensitivity in a job that dismissed such values. Feeling optimistic, Sara went over and addressed him:

"Hey, what a surprise! What are you doing here?"

"Browsing, the same as you, I suppose."

"I'm planning to take this, what do you think?" Sara's question was charged with hope, it was the perfect excuse for him to reveal himself, if her suspicions were correct. But his answer could not have been more discouraging:

"What is it, poetry? To tell you the truth, I never liked poetry very much, I could never understand it. I prefer novels, so long as they're not too demanding."

Sara quickly took her leave, trying to hide her sense of disappointment, and went over to the till. She paid for the book and left the shop, hoping to explore the treasure she held in her hands, though she was unable to do this until late in the evening, since work at the bank got absurdly complicated and she had to stay much longer than expected.

At home, next to the large window overlooking the dark sea, she discovered it was another extraordinary book. How had she managed to survive till then without reading poems that seemed to have been written with her in mind? Whose was the hand guiding her to these delicious texts? Why were they doing this? It could only be because someone had fallen in love with her and was letting her know in the most original, inspiring way possible. How long would she have to wait for her anonymous admirer to understand his messages had already achieved their target?

Over the following days, Sara carried on visiting the bookshop with a secret emotion she found difficult to keep in check. She wasn't quite sure what, but she was expecting something to happen: a new card, a different gaze, someone coming up to her with some excuse. One morning, her heart jumped into her throat when she noticed the man with the grey-blue eyes had three red roses lying delicately wrapped on the table beside him. Unable to contain her emotion, Sara raced past the cafeteria and headed for the shelf at the back. There was a new card waiting for her, a pale green card with some more wonderful verses:

But I, being poor, have only my dreams;
I have spread my dreams under your feet;
Tread softly because you tread on my dreams.

She read them through several times before turning the card over to find the book's title and author, and also her own name written in pencil so lightly it was almost invisible. *The Wind among the Reeds* by William Butler Yeats! She remembered having read some poems by this author that she liked a lot, she'd had to study him on one of the courses she took in Dublin to improve her English. She searched for the page indicated on the card and read the whole poem, which ended with the verses her unknown admirer had copied. She was so flustered she could scarcely breathe, this was the most beautiful declaration of love she'd ever read. And somehow, despite the years that had gone by since Yeats wrote these words, she knew they were also addressed to her.

She took the book and returned to the cafeteria. The man with the grey-blue eyes looked up from the newspaper he was reading and for a moment their eyes met. But it was only for a few seconds, since he immediately focused on a point behind her, smiled openly and rose to greet a woman in a red dress, with long, straight hair, who had just come into the shop. Sara stepped back and leaned against the counter. From there she watched as the two of them sat down at the table, the joy of each other's company lighting up their faces. They kissed each other very tenderly, their hands flying out to each other like birds eager to be reunited. Then he handed her the flowers and they didn't move, whispering to each other, oblivious to anything that didn't directly concern them, as if an invisible bubble had cut them off from the real world. At that moment, Sara wished she could disappear, become invisible; her suffering and discomfort were plain to see. She paid for the book with lowered head, unable even to look at the man at the till, and walked out. She decided not to go back to the bank, all she needed right now was to return home, she would call from there to say she felt suddenly indisposed.

Back in the safety of her flat, she read Yeats' poem over and over again, until she knew it by memory. She felt these words could also be hers, she too had spread her dreams under the feet of this stranger who seemed to know her so well. Suddenly a terrible thought crossed her mind. What if all this was nothing more than a joke, a cruel trick devised by her colleagues at the bank? They may have been annoyed when she stopped going out with them, perhaps they'd used someone she didn't know to leave her messages and make fun of her discomfort. Was this a subtle way to marginalize her?

She was absent from the bank for two days, claiming to be unwell. When she returned on the third day, she again went to have coffee with the other directors, as she'd always done. They were delighted to see her, no one could have said they weren't pleased to regain her company. Sara spent the whole time that day studying their faces, searching for a sign that her suspicions might be correct. A look, an ambiguous sentence... But she found nothing out of place, only the absurd suspicions her imagination created.

And so it carried on. She didn't return to the bookshop, she felt unable to do so, as if it were one of those forbidden places we try in vain to banish from our memories. At night, when she came back tired from work, she would seek refuge in the books of poems she'd collected during that brief period, especially those that had come to her through the cards. They were the secret haven she hurried to each night, a haven of words to dispel the sadness that sometimes grows in us and threatens to drown us.

At seven o'clock Pablo locked the door of the bookshop and lowered the shutter that protected the windows. Sara hadn't come to the shop that day either, she hadn't appeared in almost two weeks. The first few days he'd thought she might be unwell, but one morning he'd seen her come out of the bank and head to a nearby café with the other directors. Her absence during this time had enabled him to understand she wouldn't come back, never again would he have her so close as when she approached the till to pay for her books. Sara almost always paid by credit card, which gave him the excuse one day to stroke the skin of her hand with his fingertips as he returned the card to her, a gesture that seemed casual and filled him with sensations as intense as they were difficult to forget. He'd fallen for her the first time she'd entered the bookshop, he'd never experienced anything similar, there was so much tenderness disguised under her confident outward appearance. And then, when he'd seen the books she bought, he'd understood this was the woman he'd always dreamed of.

On arriving home, he gazed sorrowfully at the cards he'd prepared for the coming days. They were scattered all over the table, like love letters addressed to no one, pieces of paper that had once been full of wonder and were now weighed down with sadness. He decided to burn them, he didn't need to wait to be sure that Sara wasn't coming back. He found a metal tray, on which he placed the cards. He then lit a match and set fire to them. He stood there, without moving, as he read some of the verses twisting in the flames, vainly attempting to escape being burned; the same verses he'd patiently selected from some of his favourite books, searching for words he could make his own:

Your voice is slender as a kiss.

I want only to lie on your body
like a lizard drawn to the sun in days of sadness.

I send out red signals across your absent eyes.

The curve of your eyes embraces my heart.

I want
to do with you what spring does with the cherry trees.

The only card he kept back was one he'd planned to give Sara the day he summoned enough strength to slip it into the book she was buying; that way, when she discovered it, she would know he was the only one who could have hidden the cards. It contained a few lines from a wonderful novel, a few lines he found as intense as the best of poetry, which perfectly described the emotion he'd felt on seeing Sara for the first time. This Sara who may never enter the bookshop again, but who, against all hope, would remain forever in his heart:

And then Grace Tebbetts walked into the room. About five minutes into her visit, she removed the jacket and draped it over the back of her chair, and when I saw her arms, those long, smooth, infinitely feminine arms of hers, I knew there would be no rest for me until I was able to touch them, until I had earned the right to put my hands on her body and run them over her bare skin. Grace's eyes were blue. They were complex eyes, eyes that changed colour according to the intensity and timbre of the light that fell on them at a given moment, and the first time I saw her that day in Betty's office, it occurred to me that I had never met a woman who exuded such composure. As I sat with her that first day, looking into her eyes and studying the contours of her lean, angular body, that was what I fell in love with: the sense of calm that enveloped her, the radiant silence burning within.

Paul Auster, *Oracle Night*

A Radiant Silence

AUGUST LOVE

You will [kiss her]. It will be the kiss by which
all others in your life will be judged and found wanting.
Scott Hicks, *Hearts in Atlantis*

My story took place in the summer of 1968. I was
seventeen back then and worked for the Bordelle
family, who ran the only garage in town worthy of the
name. I'd been employed there for over a year and was
very proud to be able to bring home a weekly wage. I'm
aware now there were lots of important things happening
in the world at the time, in cities such as Paris or Prague
young people had taken their revolution to the streets,
but I didn't know all this back then. Vilarelle was a place
where everything seemed as fixed and predictable as
the passing of the seasons. A place where time, if it went
by at all, went by differently, though now I wonder if it
wasn't caught in the mill pond, whose water we could
never bathe in because the surface was covered in a
layer of scum that stuck to the skin like an illness.

I left school at thirteen, at home they told me I was
big enough and didn't need to learn anymore. The
senior class teacher was half deaf, but he was a good
man and fond of me. He always said I should carry on
with my studies, take my exams independently, he may
have seen I liked to read and wasn't incompetent when
it came to writing. But things being what they were, it
was like telling a young lad now to travel to the moon

on a space rocket! Absolute madness! The poor knew back then what they had in store, the few who carried on studying came from rich families. Most of us boys, as soon as we were fifteen, looked for somewhere to earn a living and acquire a trade, that's the way it was. But I'm not complaining. What's done is done, whining won't help. Besides, if I think about it, I was lucky; compared to others who ended up on a construction site or working the land for a day's pay, I got off lightly. I'd always liked cars and enjoyed going to work from the beginning. I was skilful and learned quickly. And the eldest Bordelle son, Ramón, who was in charge of the garage, was happy with what I did. He talked of paying me like the other mechanics and never tired of telling me I had a future in the car business.

Laura was Ramón's youngest daughter. She was a year younger than me, I'd known her all my life, had often seen her walking about with such skinny legs we called her "Bony Moronie" after the song by Larry Williams, which was always being played on the radio. When she turned eleven, she was sent to a convent boarding school in Coruña. She must have been the first girl from the town to go and study elsewhere. That was when I lost track of her. I suppose she came back in the holidays, but she probably hung around with the other rich kids, we poor people kept to ourselves. The truth is I didn't pay her any more attention until that summer, which is when her body changed, she became a woman and attracted all the attention.

She sometimes came into the garage, almost always to ask her father for money. I couldn't take my eyes off her, she was the most beautiful girl imaginable. She must have spent the month of July on the beach, a habit that was becoming fashionable among rich people, and was tanned like the women you only ever caught sight of in magazines or the cinema. She obviously paid no attention to me. I was just an employee who moved between cars with oil-stained hands.

The town's festivities were held in the first half of August and lasted several days. We boys waited for them with an eager anticipation that is difficult to understand nowadays. Boys now have freedoms we could only dream of, they dance and walk out with girls any day of the week, but for us the festivities were our only opportunity. The dances were held in the open and everyone attended, poor and rich alike, though there was still an invisible barrier keeping everyone in their place.

On the last night, I saw Laura with her friends, sitting outside the casino club. She was resplendent, I'm not joking, I can see her now in that white dress she was wearing, which contrasted with the tan of her body. The casino club was forbidden territory. I knew the rich kids, those on holiday, kept their distance. Even so, I plucked up the courage and went over to where they were sitting. Her friends stared at me in astonishment, aware that I was breaking an unwritten law, but I ignored them and focused my gaze on Laura's eyes:

"Do you want to dance?" I asked her.

Before she opened her lips, I knew she was going to say yes, I saw it in the look she gave me. I was a tall, handsome boy; wearing smart clothes, as I was that night, I had no reason to feel inferior to the rich kids who spent all their time idling about.

We wandered away from the bar and went down to the avenue of trees. We danced one piece after another, merging with the other couples in the clearing. We were both quite chatty and soon became immersed in each other's eyes and conversation. She remembered me, I was surprised to learn she preserved an image of me when I was a child. She made no reference to my work or her father's garage, she may have known nothing about it. And I didn't say anything, we had plenty of other things to talk about. Besides, I was ashamed of my calloused hands, so different from the soft skin of her own.

At one point, I mentioned the shower of stars. That morning, I'd read a report about it in the newspaper that had caught my attention, since it explained in great detail everything that would happen. That night was August 11th, the time each year of a phenomenon people refer to as "the tears of St Lawrence." We call them shooting stars, but really they're particles ejected by a comet on its perpetual orbit. Comet dust, small particles that burn as they enter our atmosphere and shine for a moment, eventually disintegrating. Laura had never seen them, she was very enthusiastic and kept saying how much she wanted to.

So we left the dance and wandered down to the oak wood next to the river, where the lights of the festivities didn't reach. That night, we really did see shooting stars crossing the dark expanse, both of us leaning on a railing, Laura absorbed by the spectacle while I was captivated by her sweet aroma. At one point I put my arms around her and gave her a kiss as fleeting as one of those stars. Laura responded with a shy kiss of her own.

After these innocent kisses to begin with, we discovered more passionate ones. And we embraced, embraced as if we were alone in the world and the oak wood was more than a thousand miles away from the nearest habitation. I couldn't resist the heat and scent of her body, the gentle touch of her breasts as she pressed herself against me. I was happy that night; anyone who's ever fallen in love knows the happiness I mean.

We rejoined the festivities several hours later, when the orchestra was playing the final pieces and the bars were taking in their tables. The casino club was deserted, Laura's friends must have left long before. As I walked Laura home, we didn't stop talking. We felt overjoyed, our eyes were shining, as if they still reflected the light of the stars we'd just seen. We kissed each other goodbye, promising to meet the following day.

I barely slept that night and had to get up early to go to work. I'd been in the garage for less than an hour when Ramón summoned me to his office. I thought perhaps he had some job he wanted me to do, but when I saw him close the door, I realized it was something more serious. He looked at me with a steely expression and a strange glint in his eyes.

"I'm told you were out last night with my daughter. Is that true?"

I replied it was. There was no point lying, half the town must have spotted us.

"If I ever see the two of you together again, I'll beat you so hard your own mother won't recognize you. Got it?"

I couldn't speak, this was the last thing I'd been expecting. I was so taken aback I didn't know how to react. As I was leaving, shamefaced and confused, Ramón added with ill-concealed contempt:

"You can gather your things. Go to the office and take what you're owed for the month. After that don't come back, I don't ever want to see you in this garage again."

That autumn I left for Barcelona. A cousin of mine had been there for three years and in his letters was always explaining how things were different in the city, there was all the work you could wish for. Emigrating so young was a tough experience. After all, I was barely more than a child. The endless hours on the train, which back then took a day and a half to arrive; the city noise and crowds of people in the street; the drowning sensation that came from feeling so far away from home and suddenly discovering this life thing was serious… All I wanted to do was work, to be able to start straight away was a blessing. I got a job in the same garage as my cousin, it was true there was plenty of work. I soon gained the confidence of the manager, who assigned me the most complex tasks. I already said I was quick-witted and skilled in mechanics, it was then I really learned my trade.

For the first two years, instead of hitting the town, I would spend the whole of Sunday shut up in the room I shared with my cousin, reading novels I bought in the second-hand bookshops in Sant Antoni Market and writing long letters to Laura in which I unburdened my heart. She would reply from time to time; though her letters were shorter and lacked the passion I would have liked, they helped keep up my spirits and enabled me to endure the passing of time.

After that I had to do my military service, an obligation hardly anyone got out of. I was sent to Cáceres, far away from home and work. I carried on writing to Laura from the barracks, with the same enthusiasm as in Barcelona. Or more perhaps, the hours there were endless, despite my efforts to stay busy. I received various letters from her in the first few months, but then they became less frequent and finally they dried up.

When I was discharged, I returned to Barcelona, but not to the same job. My cousin and I had taken the decision to open our own garage, with a colleague from Vilalba who was also a mechanic. We worked hard, it's never easy to make your way in life without help. But the business gradually took off and, for the first time, we were then able to arrange a rota for the summer months and take a few weeks' holiday, something most people at the time considered a luxury.

My first holiday. I could hardly believe it! Obviously I came to my home town, driving a second-hand Renault 5, the first car I'd ever had. I called Laura's house as soon as I arrived. I wouldn't be lying if I said she was happy to hear me and to know I was back in Vilarelle. We arranged to meet in a bar in the main square, the only decent place that remained open.

As I watched her walk towards me, all my dormant sensations were rekindled. She was still very pretty, more so than in some of the photos she'd sent me, and had filled out. I was happy to have her at my side, as vibrant and joyful as I'd imagined her, though there was a certain distance about her that disturbed me.

"You know?" she said after we'd been chatting for some time. "I burned all your letters, I hope you don't mind. Miguel is very jealous, I don't even want to imagine the scene he'd make if he ever discovered them."

I fell silent, not knowing what to say. My body was still there, but my insides were crumbling like a sandcastle that has been hit by a rogue wave. Laura, oblivious to what was happening, went on:

"Miguel's my fiancé. I'm sure you remember him. He was the notary's eldest son. He studied law and has just opened a lawyer's office in Coruña."

Since I remained mute, crushed by the pain I was feeling, she added:

"If you've still got them, you can burn mine as well. After all, it was mostly nonsense."

I need hardly say I didn't burn them. Not then, nor when I married Montse and the children were born and started growing up. Her letters were always with me, stored like a treasure in a vault. I carried on returning to Vilarelle each August, sometimes with my family, sometimes on my own. My father passed away, and then my mother, and my sister and I shared out the modest inheritance. I kept the house, I may have needed an excuse to make the journey. The years went by, as they do, though one doesn't quite know where one's life has gone, until this summer, when I turned fifty-six.

Today is August 11th, an important date in the calendar of my life. I've been here since the start of the month, in this old, lonely family home I resist selling. I'm alone, Montse and the children stopped coming. I can hardly blame them, there's nothing here to tie them to the past. It may well be time for me to cut the threads

linking me to Vilarelle. Time to forget, to erase some obsessive memories.

I shall go to the oak wood tonight. It's probably the only place in the whole town that's just as I remember it, all the rest has changed. I shall find a secluded spot to watch the shooting stars again, as I've been doing all these years. And that's when I shall set fire to Laura's letters.

It'll be wonderful to watch how the flames consume the words, how the smoke and sparks float upwards, as the stars pass overhead with their ephemeral glow. Stars, words, smoke: all that's left of a love that once burned in my heart as a teenager.

THIS
STRANGE
LUCIDITY

The time comes not to wait for anybody.
Love goes by, silent and fleeting,
like a night train in the distance.

Joan Margarit, *The First Cold*

Every night we return to the same place, like puppets directed by an invisible hand. He takes up position under the magnolia, except on rainy days; when it's damp, he seeks shelter in the doorway of the hardware store, as if still afraid of catching a cold or getting a migraine, as he always used to whenever he wet his feet or head. I'm not blaming him, routines end up sticking to the skin as if they were part of us. When I think about it, everything I do is a routine. If you could see me, you'd realize, after standing by his side for a few minutes, that I always grow impatient and start running up and down the pavement, without ever leaving the area between the corner shop and the greengrocer's. Sniffing here and there, at tree trunks, lamp-posts, garage corners, building walls... My snout permanently pressed up against things in an absurd attempt to pick up a scent, since I can't smell anymore, odours have disappeared for good and all that's left of them is memory.

He stays on his feet all night, indifferent to the world going by. He only has eyes for the building opposite, more specifically for the windows on the sixth floor, which is where the Woman lives. We always arrive around dusk, so at least one of the windows is normally illuminated. If it's the right-hand one, I know she's in the lounge, possibly having dinner in front of the TV; if it's the middle one, I imagine her sitting at the desk in her study, staring at the computer screen; if it's the one on the left, which is always the last to go dark, I suppose she's in the bedroom, lying in bed and reading a novel, the way he used to.

Her lights go out early, they're rarely on any time after midnight. Some days, though, they stay on late and then he starts to get worried, you can see it in his expression. But that doesn't happen often, the lights are normally off at night. He never takes his eyes off them, as if the world were nothing more than those three dark rectangles. Meanwhile I pass the time wandering about, never going far, not that I have anywhere to go, anxiously pacing up and down the pavement, still unable to accept I can't pick up the wealth of scents that used to excite me so much. I know they're there, covering every inch of the ground, and I'm the one who's lost the capacity to detect them.

The first few days, I found it difficult to accept this change. I was vaguely aware of what was going on, but couldn't understand why the channels through which I received the sensations that made up my picture of the world were suddenly blocked, while another dimension I hadn't noticed before became open to me. This strange lucidity, this ability to fathom what was previously unfathomable, this way of relating things and drawing conclusions, this putting into words everything I experience. I didn't realize this would happen, I'd never even stopped to think about it. Perhaps it was better not to imagine anything before the time came, it would have been too terrible. It's better like this. Now that the end is coming and the final night is almost upon us, I can appreciate how the only good thing about this sentence is its expiration date, the fact it will all be over in a matter of hours.

This is how we've spent every night of the last year, the hours slipping slowly by until the darkness begins to disperse and the air fills with a clarity that obliges us to withdraw to this desolate spot where we pass our days. Him sitting on the sofa, me resting on the rug, both of us motionless, occasionally exchanging glances, possibly to confirm we're still there and not alone. A routine like that of some winter afternoons before the sentencing, except that now all we do is wait. We both know everything's changed and, while we may be surrounded by the same furniture and familiar objects, this is no longer our home, but a no man's land we occupy, waiting for the night to return, so we can take to the pavement again and renew our vigil opposite the Woman's building.

Sometimes, especially on dark winter evenings, we're lucky enough to witness her coming back home from work or one of her walks. These are the best moments, because his face lights up and he focuses all his attention on her every movement. I also get excited and try to attract her attention, though I know there's no point, since there's no sound coming out of my mouth. We both watch as she pauses in the doorway, searches for her keys, sometimes turns her head and stares in our direction, as if she could see us or otherwise detect our presence. Normally, though, she just puts the key in the lock, opens the door and disappears inside the building.

That's when I start counting slowly, not stopping until one of the windows becomes illuminated. I can reach 120 or 150, though sometimes she takes longer to go upstairs and, since I don't know how to count beyond 200, I end up getting bored; by the time I realize I'm bored, the lights have finally gone on.

I remember the first day we saw her, it was at the beach. She was sitting on a bench, reading a book with a yellow cover. I stopped beside her and she started stroking me. The truth is I hadn't stopped for her, but for the extraordinarily strong odour emanating from one of the bench legs. He was a little further behind, at the beach he always liked to let me run free, and stopped when he reached us. They started talking about me and the book in her hands. After a while, she invited him to sit down and they stayed like that for ages, totally oblivious to me. Rarely had I seen my master so happy, he was positively radiant. I don't mean he was normally a bit sullen, it would be wrong to suggest such a thing. I just mean there was a special happiness about him that day which I'd never seen.

They talked and talked, until the sun was swallowed by the sea. Then, after they'd said goodbye and the two of us had returned to the car, he put on some livelier music than he generally listened to while driving and didn't stop singing all the way. Back home, having eaten dinner almost without noticing me, he took out a green notebook and started scribbling all over it. He must have carried on doing so for quite some time because that's the last image I have of that day, before going to bed and falling asleep.

After that, they started seeing each other almost daily. First they met at the beach, but we soon began to visit other places. She was very talkative and I quickly grew fond of her, since she treated me well and paid attention to me. And also because she made him happy and this put me in an excellent mood. Happy days! Most of the time, we went on long walks in places I'd never been to. I particularly remember a path between some oak trees, with the sun filtering through the leaves and lighting up small spots on the ground, so bright and warm I had to keep stopping at them. What a feast of unfamiliar fragrances! I was used to city smells, which while pleasant were always predictable, and was confused by these wilder, more piercing odours, traces of animals hiding not far away, in among all that silence. I remember another afternoon by the river, with the water bubbling along and me desperately trying to catch the butterflies that alighted on the flowers in the riverside meadows. It was the first time I'd seen so many, with such different colours, and I didn't know which one to chase. I spent half the afternoon wasting my time, since they always flew off just as I was about to reach them. I also remember from that day the hum of the crickets and grasshoppers that leaped away as I raced towards them through the tall grass. Meanwhile the two of them sat on a log, holding hands, smiling tenderly, as if they were alone in the world and nothing else mattered. I remember another morning, climbing a hillside along narrow paths between wild gorse and broom, the three of us panting from the effort. Then, at the top, my amazement at the vastness of the world stretching out over valleys in a patchwork of fields, woods and farmland. Happy times! I would feel a twinge of nostalgia right now, if it were possible for me to feel such a thing under these conditions.

One day the Woman came to our house for lunch. From early that morning, our routine was smashed to smithereens. The only thing that didn't change was our brief walk around the neighbourhood shortly after we got up. On our return, the tranquillity we normally enjoyed on his days off simply vanished. The artificial flowers in the vase in the hallway disappeared to be replaced by a bunch of freshly cut white roses. The lounge was cleaner than it had ever been, and that included my favourite rug, where I often used to doze. The table was covered in a light blue cloth I'd never seen. Two places were set, plates and glasses carefully arranged, together with a small jar holding a yellow rose. The aromas emerging from the kitchen, the scent of meat that used to drive me so crazy, had me on edge the whole morning.

I wasn't expecting to go out again before lunchtime, but quickly recovered from my surprise once I was in the open air and realized we were heading for the park with the yellow benches. I always liked going, especially on days like this, when there were fewer cars and everyone seemed to have agreed to take their dogs for a walk. As we wandered between trees and bushes that were positioned to protect the flower beds, I kept an anxious eye out for the brown-haired bitch I liked so much. There were setters, spaniels, mastiffs, westies, but that morning she wasn't among them. I was very sorry, I rarely had a chance to sniff her and run around with her, but I soon got over it and started playing with every dog I came across, that's how spontaneous I was back then.

I was panting by the time we got back home, it had been a very long walk. We'd just come in when she arrived, with that happy expression that made her different, a happiness that always influenced my master. I soon discovered the treasure in the oven was not for me. Having placed the meat tray on the kitchen surface, he began to cut thin slices, which he put in a serving dish and proceeded to drape in thick, golden gravy. He then took the dish into the lounge, while I got meatballs as usual. I wolfed them down, I was that hungry, and, as happened most days, soon fell asleep.

When I woke up, the lounge was empty. The remains of the meal were still on the table and I had to resist the urge to jump up and take a piece of meat, I knew he wouldn't like it. Besides, my attention was drawn to the noise and muffled laughter coming from my master's bedroom. I ran towards it, but found the door closed. This surprised me, the doors in our house were never closed. "Off you go, Argos, back to the lounge." His order was obscured by the Woman's giggles. I left with my tail between my legs. I'd never felt so humiliated, he'd never done this to me before. It took them some time to emerge. When they did, they both had a strange glazed look on their faces and were clearly sharing something that didn't include me.

There were many days like this. On others, having taken me for a longer walk than usual, he would leave me alone at home. I shouldn't have minded, I was used to him doing this whenever he went to work, but I was sad it happened on precisely those days we used to spend together. It wasn't difficult to guess where he'd gone, the look on his face when he came back was the same he had when the two of them spent the afternoon shut up in his bedroom. So, although it hurt spending so many hours without his company, my pain was softened by the great joy in his eyes when he returned, a joy that drove him to play with me as when we were first together.

Now that I have a better understanding of things and can reflect on my previous life, I recall the many hours I spent alone at home. They struck me then as boring, I waited anxiously for my master to return, but now I realize they could have been just as interesting as the hours we spent out walking, despite the fact they all passed between the four walls of our building.

In the mornings, we always got up early, however dark it was in winter, and quickly headed outside. We'd go for a short walk in the neighbouring streets, never going further than the entrance to the park. I loved these walks. The streets would be crawling with dogs, since lots of other people took their dogs out at the same time. This was my chance to see the brown dog with the attractive scent. Some mornings, depending on whether they let us off the leash or not, we could sniff each other to our hearts' content and even race along the pavement. But these moments were fleeting, or so they seemed to me, as if happiness in life were always limited to small doses guaranteed never to satisfy our longing.

After that, we'd return home. He'd soon head for work and I'd be left alone. As the doors were normally never closed, I could come and go as I pleased through

50

the different rooms. Some mornings, the cleaning lady would arrive and then, for a few hours, everything was much more fun, she was like a whirlwind and never stopped moving and singing. "Goddamn dog," she would complain at times, "your hair is all over the place!" But I knew she didn't really mind, you could tell from her tone of voice. I would run along behind her, from one room to the next, clinging to her skirt until I grew tired and flopped down on top of the rug. It calmed me, knowing she was there, dogs of my breed aren't used to loneliness. Maybe that's why I found the mornings the cleaning lady didn't come so hard to endure. Too many hours spent in silence, when time itself seemed to grind to a halt.

It occurs to me now how silly I was, there were plenty of things to occupy my attention. The house was silent, okay, but not the rest of the building. Noises came from other apartments, which I learned little by little to recognize. The child above us crying, the muffled sound of the television that was always on in the room next to our lounge, the trills of the canary downstairs, the music coming from one of the interior windows… I could hear these things clearly if I went into the kitchen or spare bedroom, both of which looked out onto the light well at the back. Light well! That's ironic. Light was the last thing to reach this confined space, which may have been why I preferred to stay in the lounge, listening to the monotonous sounds of the street outside. The cars, their horns, sudden braking. The rumble of a machine, the hustle and bustle of people. Noises that in winter would sometimes be silenced by the raging wind and rain beating against the windows.

The noises in the building were made by people who, like me, had stayed at home while others went to work. They were almost always women, who insisted on cooking when the sun was high in the sky, creating a stream of odours that reached my nostrils even when the windows were closed and kept me on tenterhooks until my master's return. Now that I think about it, I feel nostalgic for those days. If I could relive them, I would pay attention to the sounds of life I previously ignored.

One day, my master returned home in a pool of sadness. It's the only time I remember him walking straight past me and shutting himself in his room. He didn't come out for ages. This had me worried and confused, I didn't know what to do. It was obvious something serious had happened, but I had no idea what it was. I ended up howling next to the door of his bedroom, I couldn't bear it. He opened the door and finally acknowledged my presence, holding me close and bursting into tears.

The days that followed were terrible. I never found out what had happened, but understood he'd broken it off with the Woman. She wouldn't be coming round anymore, and we wouldn't be going around to her place either. There would be no more walks along the beach or in the country. Sadness became a permanent fixture in our home, music was silenced, walks were shorter and duller. Such bitterness! He again paid attention to me, I could spend all the hours I liked at his side, but this didn't make me feel any better, his sadness was like a cloud over our lives.

As the weeks went by, his sadness decreased. Perhaps there's truth in the saying "time heals all wounds." One afternoon, the music went back on, though only sad, melancholy songs. Our walks got longer and I suspect at the time he was happy to have me around and so feel obliged to take me out every day.

Over the following months, three women came into his life. One of them was very nice, whenever she entered the house, it was as if an earthquake was making even the tiniest object vibrate. How I longed for my master to shut himself in his room with her as well! I wanted to hear that laughter again, see the same sparks of happiness in his eyes. But it never happened and none of these women lasted very long. Soon it was just the two of us again.

After the last of these relationships, he renewed his habit of leaving town from time to time, as we had done when I was young. I enjoyed travelling in the car, though I didn't like being confined to the back seat. It was pleasant watching the world go by, understanding how much more there was to discover. Our destination was always the house of his mother, a white-haired woman who treated me well and handed me treats. It was impossible not to love her. We would return home in the evening, happy at the good time we'd had.

I remember the last of those days, how could I forget it? It was autumn now and the morning was magnificent. We walked beside the river and then went to his mother's for lunch. Later, on the way back, he decided to leave the main road and take a detour in search of a place he used to visit as a child. When we got out of the car, I discovered it was an old chestnut grove. The ground was covered in dry leaves and a large number of burs. Burs I was seeing for the first time and had to be careful of, their spikes were very painful. Some of them were half open and revealed the chestnuts held inside. My master went to the car to get a plastic bag, where he placed the chestnuts he had collected. I hadn't seen him so enthusiastic in a long time, as if this childhood activity were returning the smile he'd lost due to the absence of the Woman he continued to love. I also let myself go and didn't stop jumping up around him, I've already said I was easily influenced by the happiness of others.

Dusk was falling when we got back in the car. The sky that had been blue in the morning was now covered by thick, black clouds. Lightning flashed in the distance, illuminating the heavens with its disturbing glare. And then came the sound of thunder, a long rumble drawing gradually closer, which made my heart sink. It started raining, more and more persistently. The windscreen wipers couldn't get all the water off the glass. The road was unmarked and it was difficult to know which way to go, my master kept complaining he couldn't see a thing. That was when two strong lights appeared in front of us, flooding the inside of the car. I only had time to hear a terrible noise and then I fell into a darkness that swallowed up the lights, the car, the rain and everything around me. That blackness devoured everything, including him.

The dawn is coming. The bedroom light has just gone on. She is waking up to another day, though today is special. I wonder if she'll remember what date it is today, it's been a year since he and I abandoned this world. Though I should say "started to abandon this world," since there's this delay neither of us was expecting, these 365 days of the strange life we've been given to bid farewell to our loved ones before we vanish.

I watch my master standing motionless like a statue, eyes fixed on the rectangle of light. As I watch him moving his lips, I know he's speaking his final words, possibly some of those verses he liked so much and used to recite to me:

Thanks I would like to give
for the days you share with me,
for caresses and kisses.

I see something like a tear sliding slowly down his cheek, which accentuates the expression of infinite sadness on his face.

An older woman approaches on the pavement, accompanied by her dog, a black fox terrier. On reaching us, the animal stops and sniffs around the area where I am. I notice the confusion on his face. He's obviously aware of my presence, but can't see me or smell me. This is a sign that something of me, however small, is left in the world. I want to bark, reward his attention, but no sound comes out, we ghosts can't bark. Our presence, I realize now, is a terrible punishment, reminding us of the things we've lost.

The fox terrier continues on his way. The tugging on his leash gets stronger and forces him to leave. I look in the direction of my master, who has become a hazy figure, as if his body were disintegrating. I watch as he turns into filaments of strange mist that merge with the morning air. He still has time to look away from the window and glance at me for a split second, long enough for our eyes to meet for the last time.

Then I notice he's not the only one disappearing. Everything around me is turning into a grey, uniform mist that makes it more and more difficult to discern things. Trees, houses, lamp-posts, cars, clouds, everything is falling apart. Finally, reaching the end of that strange lucidity that has accompanied me for the past year, I understand what's really happening is that my body's beginning to fade, dissolving in a succession of threads that loosen the knots tying them together and disperse as the light of day grows stronger. I realize this year of a strange life is coming to an end for me as well, never again shall I be present in this world I loved so much. My head is being emptied of words, I can't string together enough sentences to express how grateful I am for the days I've lived. The only sentences I retain are those of the poem my master liked to recite:

Thanks for youth and senses.
Thanks for the wind that makes us strangers to ourselves.
Thanks for the sea, absolute and powerful.
Thanks for silence and verses.

A Ghost Story

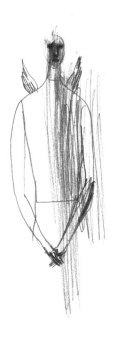

One day we will meet
on the other side of the shadow of sleep.

José Ángel Valente, *Interior with Figures*

The story I want to tell happened some time ago. If I haven't said anything until today about my experience that summer evening in an isolated boarding house in Navarre, it's because of the fear I have of everything that somehow reminds us the real world is not as solid and organized as we would like to think. There may be zones of shadow we know nothing about, mysteries that defy definition, areas we only ever glimpse by chance. In the life of every human being, there are unsettling moments, brief visions that help us to see differently and realize how much we still have to learn about ourselves.

My story happened, as I said, in the Community of Navarre. To be more precise, it took place in a country hotel – *The Rest* I think was its name – on the outskirts of the town of Obanos, which is situated on the pilgrimage route to Santiago de Compostela. At Obanos, two parts of the route come together: the one that starts in Somport and the one that begins in Saint-Jean-Pied-de-Port. It's a small town with buildings that still retain vestiges of its splendid medieval past. As you approach along roads that cross the region of Valdizarbe, having left behind the steep slopes of the Mount of Pardon, you can see from afar the tall Gothic tower of the Church of St John the Baptist, the symbol of a past that is still alive at many points along the route. Life flows along it, year after year, like a secret river that preserves on its bed the memory of dead pilgrims. Footsteps on invisible footsteps.

Like most of those gathered that evening on the large patio at the back of the hotel, I'd set out from Roncesvalles six days earlier, intending to spend the whole of June walking to Compostela. The reasons that compelled me to make this pilgrimage are not relevant here. All I will say is that they had to do with a bitter period of my life I was anxious to leave behind, but they have no bearing on the story I'm about to tell.

Though I can't be sure, I seem to remember there were ten or twelve of us in that informal gathering. Most of us had met up over the preceding days, casually bumping into one another along the way, as a result of the camaraderie there was between pilgrims. The belief that the pilgrimage route helps create friendships is true, going on my experience. Though some of us preferred to spend most of the time walking alone, we had got into the habit of planning the next stage of the route together and agreeing where we would stay the next night.

That afternoon I'd been very tired when I reached the hotel, I'd found the stretch from Pamplona more arduous than other days. Having had a shower and put on some clean clothes, I was very much in the mood to go to bed and sleep until the following day, but I resisted the temptation and went downstairs to have supper. In the dining room, I sat next to a couple from Vitoria who were doing the route in the company of their daughter, a shy girl who appeared very uncomfortable among so many older people and who limited herself to answering any questions she was asked with monosyllables. After dinner, Pere, a lawyer from Catalonia who was the leading member of the group, suggested we have a coffee out on the patio. The hotel was located in the outskirts of the town, next to a large pine grove, and had a terrace at the back that must have been frazzled by the sun during the day, but at night was extremely pleasant, with a fresh breeze that wafted the thick smell of the pines' resin in our direction.

We sat around four tables we had brought together. I felt well in the company of these people I knew so little about, but who aroused in me feelings of warmth and trust due to our shared circumstances. Though we never discussed such personal themes, I was sure they all had strong reasons for devoting the month of June to crossing the peninsula on foot, in search of that European Land's End only I had ever been to.

I remember the evening passed in predictable fashion. Sometimes the conversation would peter out but, as with a fire when you throw on some kindling, it would flare up again with another person's contribution, as if nobody present really wanted the evening to come to an end. Stories, anecdotes, experiences... Usual, everyday topics weren't mentioned at all, as if they were considered out of place. Had it not been for our clothes and the objects around us, we could easily have been mistaken for a gathering of medieval pilgrims. After all, the stars twinkling overhead were the same as those that had accompanied pilgrims since they first started seeing in the Milky Way a route traced in the sky guiding them to Compostela a thousand years earlier.

We'd been sitting under the stars for quite some time and the conversation was again threatening to peter out when one of the gathering, a thin, talkative woman with cropped black hair, went and confessed she was a poet. No sooner had she said this than several of the group began insisting she recite some of her poems. And, as I feared, it didn't take much to convince her. She read out four or five poems that struck me as mediocre, made up of words I'd heard a hundred times before. However, I joined in the applause, I didn't want to spoil the charm of such an evening.

At the end of her impromptu recital, Pere the lawyer suggested we each read out our favourite poem. Part of the group responded enthusiastically to this idea, perhaps because the anonymity of the pilgrimage route helped everybody cast aside their inhibitions. What followed was a mix of everything, from one absurd performance of Espronceda's "Song of the Pirate," probably learned at school, to the inevitable romantic verses of Neruda's *Twenty Love Poems and a Song of Despair*. When it was my turn, even though I had no wish to take part, I announced I had a sad poem it might be better not to include. At the others' insistence, I explained it was a text by José Ángel Valente, my favourite poet, a composition I continue to like today, taken from *Fragments from a Future Book*, a posthumous work written when he knew death was at his heels:

What sadness to die, reach out to you,
kiss you desperately
and sense the mirror
does not reflect my face,
unfelt by you
whom I loved so much, my
longing without presence.

My recital was followed by a long silence. For a moment, I felt guilty for having spoiled such an enjoyable evening, my verses had clearly been at odds with the otherwise festive atmosphere. And then a man who had previously remained silent spoke up for the first time. I can't say anything about him, I'd never set eyes on him before. But his presence didn't surprise me, he must have been a solitary walker who'd latched onto some members of the group during the day.

"There's a friend of mine who'd like those verses by Valente," he whispered. "It's funny. Were it not for the fact we've never met, I'd think they were based on events that happened to her. A very sad story, as all love stories are in the end."

He fell quiet and lowered his head, as if apologizing for his words. If what he'd meant was to attract the group's attention, he more than succeeded, since there were soon several voices pressing him to tell his story. After a few moments' hesitation, he succumbed to the pleas of those around him. Having waited for us to fall silent, with the same slow voice he'd employed before, he began…

"This story, as I told you just now, happened to a dear friend of mine. I'm not going to bore you with details, except to say it took place four years ago and is somehow related to the pilgrims' road, since it all began with an accident near where we are now. Diana, my friend, had just married the boy she'd been in love with ever since she was a teenager. Hers was one of those love affairs that start as an idealistic fling and end up as strong and solid as a hundred-year-old tree.

"They lived in Puente la Reina, a few miles away from here, though she worked in Pamplona, the city we left today. One afternoon when her husband had the day off, Diana urged him to come and meet her from work. They could go to the cinema and then dine out, it was an opportunity to change their daily routine. He readily agreed, nothing gave him greater pleasure than seeing the bright flame of happiness in his wife's eyes.

"Coming home, after night had fallen, the car skidded on an oil patch left by a lorry a few hours before, right at the start of the bridge over the river Arga. Out of control, the car slammed into the parapet, breaking it and falling into the river. The bridge wasn't that high, the accident could have been no more than a fright, but there are times fortune is against us. Despite wearing a seatbelt, her husband banged his head on the steering wheel; according to the coroner's report, his death would have been almost instantaneous. She was lucky. Though knocked out by the impact with the windscreen, she was soon revived by the cold water. Guided by her instinct, she managed to take off her seatbelt, wind down the window, escape through the hole and swim to the riverbank.

"Diana saved her life, but her husband didn't. It's easy to imagine my friend's sorrow, a sorrow that led her to abandon her work and withdraw to the house they'd both chosen when they decided to live together, a simple construction on the edge of town. She had no wish to see anybody and spent all her time overwhelmed by the huge sadness she felt inside. Her only companion was Daedalus, an Irish setter they'd acquired shortly after getting married. It used to be her husband who looked after it; now it was Diana's turn, and she attended to its needs with a special tenderness, as if this were a way to keep alive the memory of a love affair cut short by the accident.

"After two months' isolation, she decided one day to get on with her life, she couldn't let her sadness prevail. She found a part-time job in an office in town and adopted certain daily routines, in the vague hope these changes would eventually help her regain the will to live.

"Over the next few weeks, she did what she could to overcome her pain and tackle life with renewed energy. Her work kept her busy in the mornings; in the afternoons, she would go for long walks in the country, with Daedalus at her side. These outings exhausted her and enabled her to fall asleep during the difficult hours of the night. At home, she was in the habit of talking aloud, as if her husband were still there, though she knew she was alone and these directionless words were aimed at breaking the silence that weighed her down. She liked to pretend her husband was in the house, attending to some chore, while she busied herself in the kitchen or lounge that held their books. Sometimes, when she went upstairs, a familiar sound such as a door closing, a creak, the noise of a car stopping nearby, encouraged her to believe he was still alive and would appear before her at any moment.

"She sought refuge in reading, as so many people do at difficult stages of their lives. Novels took her attention, especially at night, when sleep eluded her. But during the day she preferred poetry and kept a book by one of her favourite authors always close at hand. There was one book, however, she couldn't find: *Point Zero*, a 1972 publication in which José Ángel Valente collected all the poems he'd written up until that date. It was a wonderful edition, like all those produced by Barral Editores, with a cover showing an image, reproduced like the stills of a film, of a crow perching on a book, pecking at the ink that had spilled out of an inkwell. Her husband had given it to her, having discovered it in a second-hand bookshop, knowing the weakness she had for such things. She'd searched all over the house, but not found it anywhere. She could buy a new edition, another publisher had just reissued the book, but she wanted this one that was so special to her, full of the notes and scribbles she'd left in the margins.

"Diana found it normal to have the feeling her husband was still with her. Don't they say when we lose a limb, we carry on feeling it as if it were still there? How much more then a beloved person, especially when the union was as strong as theirs? An absence is difficult to overcome, you have to give it time, was her friends' advice. But as the weeks went by, instead of decreasing, the sensation her husband was in the house began to grow. She put it down to loneliness,

perhaps she shouldn't have insisted on staying in a house that was too big for one person. She often found herself climbing upstairs, or rushing downstairs, with a mixture of desire and fear, but always with the hope her husband was waiting. Sometimes, when preparing something in the kitchen, she'd feel his presence behind her and turn around, hoping for a moment she could kiss him. But there was never anyone there, just the void she'd lived with since the day of the accident.

"She would wake at night in a panic, surrounded by darkness, thinking there was someone else in the room, sitting on the chair or at the foot of her bed. She would remain motionless, not daring to switch on the light, holding her breath, pricking up her ears, trying to capture the sound of a sigh or rustle that betrayed a foreign presence. But when she finally turned on the light, there was no one there and she was as alone as when she'd gone to bed.

"One day, on coming back from work, she found a bunch of carefully arranged red roses in the crystal vase in the lounge. She immediately thought of the cleaning lady who came twice a week. What could have prompted such a gesture? She certainly didn't remember having told her these were her favourite flowers. And yet this was the only logical explanation, though she was powerless to prevent another, more absurd but more forceful explanation gathering strength in her mind. She knew it was impossible, the only two people who could have put those flowers there were herself and the cleaning lady. But had it been her, she would have remembered. Or would she? She was afraid she was going mad, losing touch with reality, she knew loneliness and sorrow could do this to someone.

"She tried not to become too obsessed with what had happened. She even determined, from that point on, to write down the things she bought, the changes she made in the house. That way, she'd make sure her memory didn't start playing tricks on her.

"One afternoon, on the way back from their daily walk in the country, Daedalus took off and ran towards the house, which was still fifty yards away. He ran and barked with sudden joy, as if a very dear person were waiting for them inside. He stopped anxiously in front of the door while she scrabbled in her pockets for the key. When she finally managed to open the door, the dog made straight for the lounge with all the enthusiasm of when her husband was alive. Not knowing what to do, Diana stood in the doorway, watching Daedalus exit the lounge and search all the rooms, confused by the contrast between reality and what his senses told him.

"She also went round the different rooms, though she knew there was nothing in them, no one could have entered the house in their absence. That evening, a sudden impulse made her search for Valente's book again. She had a keen desire to reread some of his poems, she knew from experience they would help her relax. It had to be hidden on one of the shelves, it wouldn't be the first time a book had been staring her in the face without her realizing. She scanned the shelves from top to bottom. Nothing there! She then went to the garage, where there were still some sealed boxes from the move. She opened them and emptied them out, but her search was in vain. Of course it could also be at her parents' house, she'd left several books there when she first got married.

"She decided to visit them the following Saturday, she hadn't seen them in weeks. Over lunch, she adopted an expression of joy she didn't feel, the last thing she wanted was for them to detect her sadness. Then, when her mother was tidying up and her father dozing in front of the TV, she went through her old bedroom, and the shelves in the living room, in search of the edition of *Point Zero* she so desperately wanted to recover. But the book wasn't there. She didn't know how she could have lost it, she didn't recall having lent it to someone, she never lent such personal books. There was nothing for it but to accept she would have to buy a new edition, knowing it wouldn't be the same, the books we love carry the memory of us and our dreams on their pages.

"Towards evening, Diana took her leave of her parents. It was getting dark and she didn't want to have to drive at night. During the journey, she felt her heart heavier than usual, it had been difficult to conceal her pain for so many hours. When she entered the house, Daedalus was overjoyed to see her. But what caught her attention more than the dog's affection was the slight aroma of perfume pervading the house. It was the same her husband had once used, a male fragrance she was all too familiar with. How was this possible?

"She went to the bathroom. The door of the bottom cabinet, which is where she'd put all her husband's toiletries, since she hadn't been able to throw them away, was open and the bottle of perfume was missing its lid. Again she was assailed by the sensation she wasn't alone, not just because of the aroma. Something, that strange sense that had been growing inside her ever since the accident, told her there was someone else there. But she knew it was impossible, she had to control this unruly imagination that seemed to be dominating her recently.

"On leaving the bathroom, she realized it wasn't there where the smell of the perfume was strongest. It seemed to be coming from the first floor. She rushed upstairs, her heart beating wildly. As she walked along the corridor, the fragrance became more noticeable. She pushed open the bedroom door. Here the smell was at its most intense, as if all the perfume had been concentrated inside and, free at last, was now escaping into the house.

"But Diana wasn't interested in the perfume. How could she be? The whole of her being was drawn to an object lying on the quilt, the same quilt she'd spread out on making the bed that morning, before she'd left. She rushed over to pick it up, though, as soon as she saw it, her inner sense told her what she was going to find. There on the bed was her old copy of *Point Zero*, Valente's book of poems that had accompanied her over the years. She took it, struggling to contain her emotion. Her hands could barely hold it, they were trembling so much. There was a bookmark sticking out of the top. She opened the book at the page it showed and found the poem she'd often recited to her husband, those few verses that had once helped them to feel more closely connected:

Love is in what we put forward
(bridges, words).
Love is in all that we raise up
(laughter, flags).
And in what we fight
(night, emptiness)
for true love."

The man fell quiet and lowered his head, indicating the end of his story. I was greatly impressed and had lots of questions for which even he may not have had an answer, perhaps because there wasn't one. The other members of the group must have felt something similar, because no one said anything, as if we were all still pondering the details of the story we'd heard.

"It's late. If we want to leave early tomorrow, we'd better start thinking about going to bed," said Pere, getting up and heading inside the hotel.

One by one, the others followed him, until only the man and I were left. We remained in silence for a short period, staring at the strip of shadow around us. There were so many things I wanted to ask, but the expression on his face was not inviting, as if he were still absorbed by the story he'd just told. In the end, I got up as well and, having wished him good night, went to my room.

It took me a long time to get to sleep, his story had unsettled me and kept buzzing around inside my head, as did the poems by Valente, the one I'd read and the one this man had used to round off his story. I felt I'd behaved like an idiot and my shyness had again got the better of me. I wanted to talk to him for longer, it's not often we meet people who love the same poems we do.

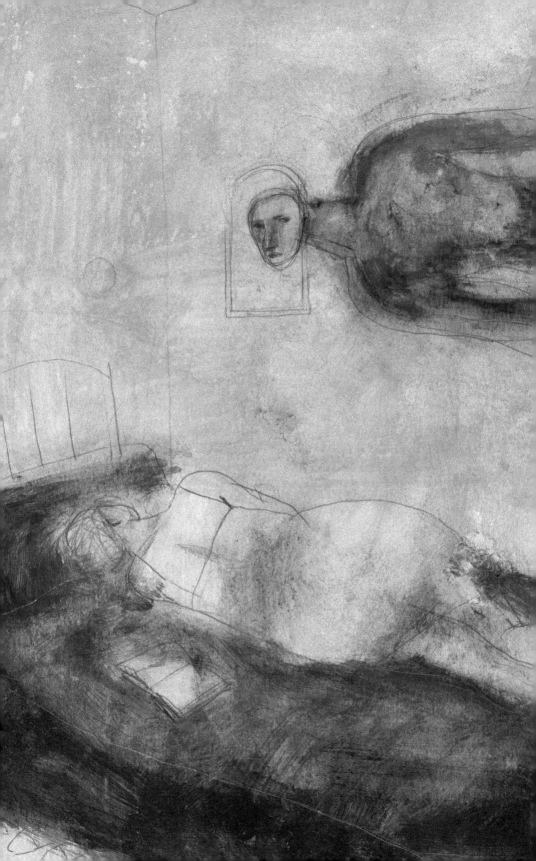

I finally managed to console myself with the thought there was still something I could do. I had to start a conversation with the stranger the following morning; perhaps we could even walk part of the way together, I wouldn't mind abandoning my self-imposed solitude for the sake of being with him.

The next day, I got up early, I wanted to be first in the dining room. When I arrived, there was no one there and I had to have breakfast on my own. I then took the newspapers and prepared to wait for the other guests to come down. My plan was to invite the man to sit with me, any excuse would do to enter into conversation.

All the people from the previous evening came down. All except the one I really wanted to see. I was perplexed and went to ask the manager if anyone had left the hotel earlier that morning. "No," he replied. "Everyone who stayed the night is now in the dining room."

His words left me feeling uncomfortable. How was this possible? I went from table to table, asking the other guests if they'd seen the man who'd told us the previous night's story. No one could tell me anything about him, though they all remembered my staying behind.

There was something unusual about all of this, and it wasn't just my frustration at not being able to talk to that stranger. I was not prepared to leave without an answer and decided to wait in the hotel. I explained to my fellow walkers that I didn't feel well, I would set out later and aim to catch up with them before they reached Estella, that day's destination.

As soon as they had left, I again sought out the manager and began a conversation. Having gained his trust, I casually enquired whether he remembered there being an accident four years before, at the point where the road crosses the river Arga.

"Sure I do! That bridge is less than a mile from here."

"Are we so close to the river? I thought it was further away."

"It was one of those meaningless accidents, it should never have happened," the man seemed genuinely upset. "There's a really clear stretch of the road there, the fact is there's never been a problem since. Such is the way of misfortune, you never know where it's going to hit you."

"I believe one person died, is that right?"

"Yes. There was a married couple in the car. He was driving, I guess he must have drowned. The woman got out through one of the windows."

I was about to ask more when the manager, after eyeing me for a moment, added:

"Listen, if you're so interested, I think I can show you the newspaper reports. We had just opened and placed an advert in the press, so I'm pretty sure I kept a few copies. Wait here for a moment."

He went to reception and opened a door in the wall on the right. It didn't lead to a room but revealed a built-in cupboard full of shelves on which were registers and folders possibly containing bills and other business documents. He took one of the folders and, having closed the door, came over to where I was.

"Here are the papers. Read them for as long as you like. All I ask is that you return them as you found them."

I accepted the material he gave me and went to sit at one of the tables on the patio, which had all been returned to their original position. It was pleasant there. The sun wasn't hot and there was a fresh breeze that would disappear in a few hours. I put the folder on the table and pulled out a few old copies of Navarre's daily newspaper.

I soon found what I was looking for. There was a four-column report about the accident on one of the inside pages, with a photograph of the place where it had happened and a smaller portrait of the person who had died: a man in his thirties, with jet-black hair and a long-drawn face, staring at me from this page that had turned yellow with the passage of time. A man identical in every way to the stranger of the previous evening with his intense, disturbing story of ghosts and love.

RIVERS OF MEMORY

Such bitter rivers of memory.

Antonio Martínez Sarrión

Having left a narrow, winding road behind, the car reached the top of the hill and started its descent. It was then María was able to glimpse again the landscapes she had kept for so long in her memory: the valley opening out in a mosaic of different coloured fields, reaching as far as the horizon and the line of the sea; the path of the river flanked by alders growing on its banks; and, down below, the town with houses in the old quarter huddled around the church. Some things had changed, the masses of eucalyptus trees were new to her which now covered the hillside and encroached on the valley where before there had been only fields. And in the town, following the direction marked by the main road, there was now a whole range of new buildings, soulless apartment blocks that reminded her of those constantly springing up in the suburbs of her city.

Despite the changes, the space in front of her was the same as that in her memory. She felt an almost childish excitement, a sudden desire to get out of the car and run down the hill, as she had done as a girl so many years previously.

She stopped herself from giving voice to her excitement, from telling her husband about the wave of emotions washing over her. It had been difficult enough to persuade him to take this detour, it didn't really matter whether they arrived in Bilbao in the afternoon or evening, there'd still be plenty of time, the Guggenheim wasn't going anywhere... He'd unwillingly agreed to abandon the convenience of the motorway and take a road that, while wider in parts, was the same María remembered from her childhood. She knew he'd only done this to indulge her whim and was sure he wouldn't turn up the chance to remind her of it later on. Her husband didn't understand, had no interest in her desire to return to this town so far off the beaten track, the kind of place people prefer not to visit because there's nothing special to see there.

María herself had been surprised by this unexpected desire that had sprouted inside her. She'd noticed it a few months before, when the tiny shoot had first taken root in her mind. She'd thought it was a symptom of old age and she had reached a time in her life when the temptation to look back was more powerful than the wish to make future plans. To begin with, she hadn't given it importance, but then the longing had grown and finally it had turned into an obsession. And when her husband had talked of making a trip to Bilbao, she'd been enthusiastic. They would pass near the town, this was the opportunity she'd been waiting for. "I spent six years there, from the age of nine to fifteen; six important years for me," she confided to her husband. "They can't have been that important if your parents never took you back there," he retorted.

It was true her parents had never gone back to the town, had even avoided mentioning its name, as if by banning it from their conversation, they would also expunge it from their memory. Once, when she'd asked about it, her mother had said they'd just passed through, had not had time to put down roots. But María's experience was different, she recalled the years she'd spent there like remains unearthed by desire. Remains that made her want to return, just as she was about to.

The car had finished its descent and was now entering the town. The town had changed, but not so much that María couldn't find her way along narrow streets that seemed somehow stuck in the past. Her husband kept glancing over at her, with a look that was both inquisitive and ironic, a smug look she knew very well and had long since stopped responding to. They reached the main square, which was almost exactly the same, and turned onto a larger road. "Stop, stop, it's here," said María, pointing to a building that towered over other, smaller houses. "That's where we used to live, number 85. Except the house was the same as the others, they must have pulled it down to construct this building." She spoke now with increasing enthusiasm, overwhelmed by a flood of sensations that were out of control. "You see that block of flats, that's where the meadow was we played in as children. Nearby was the field, the Field of the Rock we called it, because it had an enormous boulder in the middle, which rose from the ground like the petrified back of some prehistoric animal."

She stopped talking when she realized her husband wasn't listening, had no interest in her emotions. She was sorry, there was nothing she would have liked more than to share her enthusiasm with somebody, but she knew there was no point expecting this from him. "I'm going for a wander. Do you want to come?" she asked, guessing what his answer would be. Her husband gestured scornfully, said no, he preferred to stay in the car. María got out, took a narrow street leading from the square, letting herself be guided by her memory through this labyrinth of paved roads. She soon found the field she was looking for. It had changed, but this was the scene from her childhood. They'd made a park there and erected a building on the far side, but left the enormous boulder where it was, a kind of abstract sculpture surrounded by children's games.

She started walking down one of the paths that crossed the park. The further she got, the more memories came to her she thought she had forgotten. It was as if this space held the experiences she'd had over those years, as if a giant underground memory accumulator switched on in response to her footsteps.

She went over to the rock, caressed the rough surface, as she had done so often as a girl. She then sat down on a ledge in the rock and closed her eyes, picturing the scenes that poured into her mind. All experiences are buried in memory, all waiting for the moment to emerge onto the surface, she thought. It was there, on that very rock, Carlos had given her her first kiss. She remembered the St John's Eve when the two of them had escaped the bustle of the bonfire burning in the main square and touched each other in the shelter of the rock. She felt again the warmth of Carlos' lips meeting hers, the sensations provoked by his hands timidly exploring her body, stroking her nascent breasts. Carlos, what had happened to him? She hadn't seen him since, his letters had dried up shortly after they left. It was normal they each get on with their lives, theirs had been a teenage love affair, a kind of sentimental apprenticeship. Or was she wrong and in fact this had been the only true love in her life?

She felt a twinge of nostalgia she was unable to explain, this had never happened to her. She remembered the afternoon she informed Carlos they were leaving, her parents had been relocated to Coruña. A sad afternoon. Holding hands, they'd gone down to the stream and Carlos had given her a blue flower growing on the bank, a chance flower she'd appreciated more than the finest bunch of roses, the same she still kept between the pages of *The Pearl*, the book by John Steinbeck that had been a present from Carlos on her name day. A dry flower after so many years, withered like the memory of their romance.

She stood up and almost subconsciously tried to repeat the movements they'd made that afternoon. She searched for the stream. It had to be on her right, but there was nothing there. She looked around, confused not to find a stream anywhere.

A young man was crossing the park, clearly in a hurry. María stopped him and, having exchanged some pleasantries, asked him the question that was bothering her. "Didn't there use to be a stream around here?" The man lapsed into silence for a few seconds, possibly surprised by her question. "Yes, there did, the stream from the hillside," he finally answered. "It's still here, only now it goes under the park. They built a channel for it when they made the new House of Culture."

The man left. María stood there for a few minutes, not knowing what to do. She then retraced her footsteps and returned to the car, her husband would be tired of waiting. She opened the door and took her seat, moving mechanically. Her husband put down the salmon-coloured newspaper he was reading and started the engine, without saying a word. She remained in silence as well, watching as they passed through the town and left the final dwellings behind. A few unexpected tears welled up in her eyes. "Is something wrong?" her husband asked. "No," she replied. "It's the cold, you know how it always makes my eyes water." He seemed to accept her answer and concentrated on the driving, trying to make up for the time they'd lost due to that unfortunate detour. She kept quiet, though she knew it wasn't the cold that had caused those tears; if she confessed what she truly felt, it would only make matters worse.

Her childhood remained where it was, drowned in the river of time. She understood we always leave part of our lives in the places we inhabit, abandoned there like shreds of mist caught between branches of trees in the early morning. She felt there was an underground river running through her as well, a hidden, channelled river like the stream in the Field of the Rock. A channel of cold, solid cement aimed at collecting all the dreams time has seen fit to throw out.

Her husband's voice broke her reverie. He was talking of finding somewhere to eat, and the hours they still had left to travel. María struggled to stem her tears and return to normality. She glanced at her watch, forced a smile; then, pretending to work out the hours, told him not to worry, they had plenty of time and no doubt would be in Bilbao before nightfall.

In Praise

of Stamp-Collecting

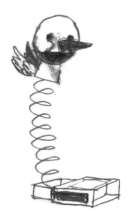

I remember I started collecting
matchboxes and cigarette packs.

Georges Perec, *Memories*

Ernesto Soutelo had collected matchboxes ever since he was a child. As often happens with such hobbies, he'd started collecting them for no particular reason, just because he wanted to have all the football badges that had appeared on Spanish matchboxes as an advertisement when he was ten years old, at the end of the 1950s. In fact, the idea of a collection came to him when he'd achieved the whole series and aroused the admiration and envy of all the other boys in his neighbourhood. An event that boosted his self-esteem and encouraged him to continue on such a promising road.

As the years went by and the field of his social relations widened, so Ernesto's chances of expanding his collection grew. This was a time when matches served an important function, both in the home and for smokers, and no one could imagine their usefulness would be reduced to the marginal place they occupy nowadays.

When he married Margarida Vilar on the feast of the Epiphany in 1979, Ernesto's collection had advanced considerably. It was difficult not to be fascinated by the wide variety of boxes he'd obtained, some made of wood, others of different types of card, boxes with an elegant, stylized design next to others that were more basic and rudimentary, discreet colours next to eye-catching images, familiar texts next to words in exotic, unknown languages. After his marriage, Ernesto began an intense correspondence with the members of a network of collectors scattered across the globe, who exchanged rare examples of these much-sought-after boxes. The collection grew and grew, as did the interest and pride of its owner.

During the first few years of their married life, Margarida adopted a warm, curious attitude towards this harmless collection. When another couple came round, she would even urge her husband to exhibit it, leading to sessions in which Ernesto could share all the knowledge he'd acquired on such an unusual theme.

The passage of time did nothing to lessen Ernesto's enthusiasm, but it did affect that of his wife, who, year after year, felt an ever stronger aversion towards these boxes that kept increasing in number, taking up more and more space in a flat that was already small. One evening, after an argument whose fierceness surprised even her, she succeeded in relegating the collection to a cupboard in the hall, freeing up the lower part of the sideboard in the lounge it had previously occupied. This banishment to the darkness of the hallway somehow signified the boxes' removal from family life. From that day on, Ernesto never made mention of his collection and only dared to bring it out when his wife was not at home.

Ernesto Soutelo died of a heart attack at the age of fifty-nine, as the first cold of autumn reached the city streets. The collection, put on hold from the day of their argument, consisted then of 1,346 boxes. After the first few weeks of obligatory mourning, Margarida decided the time had come to adapt the flat to her new circumstances. The Christmas holidays gave her the days off she required to bring herself to sort out and organize all the storage space.

One afternoon, she took the boxes her husband had patiently gathered and prepared to burn them in the fireplace in the lounge. "Can you imagine, collecting all this nonsense?" she thought to herself. "Were they stamps, at least one could sell them and make some money. But who wants empty matchboxes?" As she chucked them on the fire, revived by this unexpected extra fuel, Margarida made a quick summary of her life with Ernesto. "Almost twenty-five years together! He was a good man, but not an easy character. The headaches I've had to put up with!"

One by one, the boxes were consumed, while the fireplace filled with lively, impermanent flames. And since it's only a particular kind of carbon, the magnificent 24-carat diamond mounted on a white-gold ring burned as well, which Ernesto had hidden in one of the boxes shortly before he died, hoping to surprise his wife on their forthcoming silver wedding anniversary, in memory of the joyful score years and five they had spent in each other's company.

A Photo in the Street

The world is governed by chance.

Paul Auster, *Oracle Night*

Daniel found the first photo one Monday in the month of July, shortly before midday. It was lying on the pavement directly opposite the Vice-Chancellor's Office and he noticed it by chance. As he bent down to pick up the small rectangular piece of paper, he was able to see, as he'd already guessed, it was a passport photo. And that was when, standing in the middle of the pavement, he felt a shiver inside which caused his heart to start beating wildly. It was as if he'd suddenly been transferred to another place where reality took second stage, the people around him vanished, and all existence became him and the piece of paper. If there was a woman who embodied his ideal of beauty, it was her image he held in the palm of his hand. The photo showed only the head and a small part of the torso of the woman being portrayed, since it was cut just below the collarbone, where the breasts began to grow, but Daniel didn't mind the image being framed in this way. He didn't need to see any more, he already felt fascinated by the face he was contemplating. How to forget the intensity of those eyes?

He entered a café nearby and sat at a free table, still overcome by the impression the photo had caused.

He ordered a cup of coffee and, after the waiter had returned to his place behind the counter, he opened the palm of his hand, which had been closed till then, and continued to observe the photo. He felt that shiver again, perhaps more intensely than at first, and was amazed by the beauty smiling out at him. Because there was a smile there, though it was so faint you had to pay attention not to miss it. It wasn't in the thin-lipped mouth, half closed when the photo had been taken. No, the smile was in the eyes, big, lively eyes the colour of honey. They had a kind of ironic, mocking glint, which was what gave him the impression the woman was smiling.

It was those eyes that most attracted Daniel, though the oval of the face, flanked by shoulder-length, chestnut-coloured hair hanging straight, also struck him as perfect. He'd recently read several articles that talked of the importance of the vision of the person taking the photograph, how the eyes limit reality and choose the best moment to immortalize it. But this was just a passport photo, a routine shot by some photographer unconcerned with artistic sensibility; or else it had been the technical soul of some automated machine that had taken the photo. All the more reason to believe this woman was more wonderful in person.

Having gazed at the photo for several minutes while his coffee was left to grow cold, Daniel noticed there was a name written on the back: "Diana." Nothing else, no surname, phone number or address, just a name, "Diana," a handful of letters that gave the photo a whole new dimension. This name was a clear indication that the woman existed, he wasn't contemplating a remote, untouchable image like those in magazines, which meant she must be somewhere in the city, walking around, reading, eating, dreaming… She was real, as real as he was. And therefore there was a chance of locating her, meeting her and, if all went well, starting a relationship.

This thought presented itself with such force in his mind he felt dizzy for a moment, as if he'd lost all his bearings. He overcame his stupor and took a decision: he would find this Diana who had blazed a trail into his life. It couldn't be that difficult, Vigo wasn't such a large city. He would find her and return the photo, describing the lengths he'd had to go to; this would serve as an excellent introduction to their relationship. A relationship that would go from strength to strength, something told Daniel this wasn't just a coincidence. He knew people's lives were made up of chance happenings that can alter their existence from one moment to the next. Well, this was the stroke of luck he'd been counting on for months, perhaps without realizing. His loneliness, which had lasted longer than he would have liked, was about to end. In a way, it had already ended, because the appearance of this photo was clearly the first stage, the prelude to an affair he imagined as joyful.

Calmer now, and convinced he'd made the right decision, he set about thinking of the best strategy to locate her. The photo had been lying on the pavement opposite the Vice-Chancellor's Office, and this gave him a clue. These days, students were registering for the new university year, he'd already seen long queues outside the previous week, there'd even been a photograph in Vigo's daily newspaper. Diana must be a final-year student, her face showed she was no longer a teenager.

She'd come to register and dropped one of her photos, the same photo chance had directed into his hands.

With a determined air, he left the café and headed for the Vice-Chancellor's Office. At this hour, there was hardly anyone there, just four or five girls who kept joking with one another. He patiently waited his turn and, when it came, showed the photo to the woman on duty. He explained he was waiting for a girlfriend who was due to register that day and wanted to know if she'd already been there. The woman examined the photo Daniel held out to her and replied she didn't remember having seen her. He insisted. Perhaps she'd come earlier, when someone else was on duty. Why didn't she ask her colleagues? The woman got up patiently and showed the photo to the people working at desks nearby. They gazed first at the photo and then at him, but all shook their heads. Finally the woman returned the portrait and suggested his friend may not have arrived yet; the office was open until two, why not wait outside?

Frustrated by this early setback, Daniel left the building and wandered through the arcade on Rosalía de Castro Street, not knowing quite where to go. All his enthusiasm had suddenly vanished, as if the path opened by this photo had led to a concrete wall. He turned onto Velázquez Moreno and climbed the hill until he reached the House of the Book. He stopped for a moment to look at the novelties in the shop window, almost all of which were bestsellers he had no interest in. An older lady stopped at his side, with a brown cocker spaniel. Daniel moved away, since the dog had started sniffing his trousers with excessive zeal. And, on glancing down at the pavement, he realized there was another passport photo lying next to his shoes. He bent down to pick it up with sudden emotion. He looked at it and had to lean against the wall, breathe in and out to regain the calm he needed to persuade himself this wasn't a hallucination. There was Diana again; there she was, in the palm of his hand, eyeing him with that ironic smile he knew so well. The same photo, and the same name written on the back in identical handwriting.

How was this possible? Can a person drop two photos in a single morning? And how come no one else had spotted them? Why was it his hands they'd fallen into? He was again confronted by chance, this chance that seemed determined to give him another opportunity. Without thinking twice, he entered the bookshop and asked the cashier if the person in the photograph had been there that morning. He received a vague answer, since the cashier felt unable to say yes or no. He got the same answer from two other attendants standing between the shelves. There were always so many people coming in and out!

When he left the bookshop, the idea of locating Diana had turned into an obsession, he felt he couldn't let such an opportunity pass by. How could he find a clue that would help him move forward? It was then he remembered Anxo, one of his best friends at school. He knew he worked for the university computing services and could surely carry out the task he had in mind. Luckily he had his phone number in his diary. He rang him immediately. After the inevitable greetings and commonplaces, given that they hadn't seen each other for quite some time, Daniel explained his reason for calling:

"There's this girl who registered for university today or at the end of last week. I need to know how to locate her: a phone number, her address, e-mail, it doesn't matter. All I know is her name is Diana." Since his friend remained silent, no doubt startled by the unusualness of his request, he added, "You must have access to the university databases, you could easily find out how many Dianas registered these days. There can't be that many, it's not such a common name."

To begin with, Anxo put up a weak resistance. There was the protection of personal data, the difficulty of accessing up-to-date lists... Daniel pulled out all the stops and didn't have to insist much before convincing him. They agreed to meet that evening at the bar Van Gogh, where they could drink a few beers in celebration of their reunion.

At seven o'clock, Daniel was already sitting outside the Van Gogh, which was still half empty. His friend didn't take long to come. Time and work had distanced them against their will, so they both felt happy to be together again. They greeted each other warmly, recalling episodes from their school years and talking about their respective jobs. Daniel was keen to find out what information Anxo had brought with him and questioned him at the first opportunity:

"Here are your Dianas," Anxo handed him the folded sheets he pulled out of his bag. "I searched all the faculties, from first years to doctoral students. Whether or not you think there are many will depend on your point of view. In total, I found twenty-three Dianas."

Once he had the sheets in his power, Daniel was anxious to get away. At around eight o'clock, he claimed

A Photo in the Street

he had a subsequent meeting and had to go. Anxo didn't object, he also had several matters to attend to. They took their leave, promising vaguely to meet again, and went their separate ways.

Back at home, Daniel went through the list. Twenty-three people in all, which wasn't so many. He decided to cross out the seven Dianas who were first years, they had to be younger than the girl in the photo, but he didn't dare reject any other year. He then started thinking of a way to make contact with the remaining sixteen.

Since Anxo had only furnished him with the addresses, he drew up a new list with the names grouped according to where they lived and then worked out four itineraries that would cover all the streets on the list.

The following day, he dressed more formally, took the leather briefcase he'd inherited from his father and set out on the first itinerary. His initial plan had been to take the role of a salesman, but he soon rejected this idea. He knew people didn't like salesmen and were in the habit of slamming the door in their faces. In the end, he opted for the role of employee of a market research company conducting a survey among university students. The previous evening, he'd prepared some leaflets on the computer containing generic questions that would serve as a smoke screen for his real purpose, together with some business cards for an imaginary "21st Century Consultants" printed on cream-coloured card.

The first name on the list was Diana Soutelo Lamas, a third-year student of electrical engineering. She lived in Venezuela Street, in a building that had to be more than thirty years old. The entrance hall was spacious, with walls covered in dark wood panels and decorated with large black and white photos of the city. The lift, narrow and noisy, took him up to the fifth floor. He felt like an actor in a scene he'd watched a hundred times before on TV. In films, they never got it right the first time, but Daniel knew real life didn't have to be the same as that portrayed on the big screen. Perhaps here, behind the first door, was the woman who had captivated his heart.

An old lady opened, so large she must have had difficulties entering the rooms, unless the doors in this apartment were unusually wide. She eyed him with distrust, filling the space left by the open door.

"Good morning, I should like to talk to Diana," Daniel started, adopting a professional air.

"I am Diana," answered the woman curtly.

"Well, actually, the person I wanted to talk to is Diana Soutelo," he continued. This woman must be some relative, perhaps the girl's mother.

"That's my daughter," she replied. Then she added suspiciously, "What is it you want?"

"I'm conducting a survey on behalf of Vigo University. They wish to understand better the computing habits of university students. You know, Internet, e-mail, chats..."

"A survey? That's what another man said last week. Turned out what he really wanted was to sell us an encyclopedia that cost an arm and a leg. You wouldn't be trying to pull the same thing?"

"I'm not a salesman, madam. Do I look as if I'm selling encyclopedias? I told you I'm conducting a survey and need to ask your daughter a few questions."

The woman looked him up and down, then told him to wait and closed the door. When the door reopened, there was a young girl standing in front of Daniel, her hair tied back in a ponytail. She was wearing a pink vest and old jeans. She was attractive, yes, but had nothing in common with the girl he was seeking. Though he couldn't hide his disappointment, Daniel put into action the plan he had for such a situation. Having asked her what she was studying, he bombarded her with questions that were as general as they were easily forgettable. The girl felt like talking more than he did, so he contented himself with listening to her and pretending to jot down her answers. Ten minutes later, he was back in the street. He crossed out the first name on the list and prepared to continue searching.

That day he had no luck on any of his visits, and the following days were the same. Some of the girls were rude to him; others, unpleasant; most of them, indifferent. The worst thing of all was that none of the Dianas he met looked anything like the girl in the photo. There were three who were away from home. This made him hold out hope, but they were soon accounted for: one of them had spent the previous two weeks in her village; another was spending the summer in Galway to improve her English; the third had just gone into hospital with an appendicitis. None of them could possibly be the girl who'd dropped her photos in front of the Vice-Chancellor's Office and the bookshop.

There was nothing for it but to abandon the search he'd undertaken with such enthusiasm. It took him three days to get over his depression, which he spent shut up at home, staring at the photos of this woman he felt so close as if he'd known her all his life. In the end, he decided he wasn't going to solve anything by staying at home, he had to go out and look for her in the maze of streets, parks, cafés, shops, cinemas… Perhaps these photos were his Ariadne's thread. If chance had placed them before him, there was no reason not to think he might bump into that woman at any moment.

The day he took his search back onto the streets, he found a third photo. It was in the afternoon, on the harbour breakwater. He was tired of so much walking and wished to feel the sea breeze on his face and contemplate the stubborn battering of the waves, which were larger that day than usual. When he sat down to rest on a granite block, he noticed something only he may have seen: in front of him, mixed with earth and bits of dried seaweed, was a small piece of card he picked up with suppressed emotion. On turning it over, he felt suddenly dizzy. There was Diana's face again, a third photo that must have been lying there for several days, since it was creased and discoloured by the sun. But it was her, he had no doubt, her name was on the back, though it was so dirty the letters were barely discernible.

This was the definitive sign, it couldn't be anything else! Here was the confirmation of his future, chance couldn't be so persistent. This woman and he were destined to meet, he was absolutely sure. She might be one in several hundred thousand, but finding her was not impossible. He just had to scour the streets, not stop until he located the woman he had set his heart on forever.

So it was that, day after day, Daniel tirelessly roamed the city's streets, optimistically gazing at every woman whose path he crossed. Sometimes she looked a lot like the Diana of his dreams and, when he caught sight of her in the distance, his heart went into turmoil. But then she passed nearby and a black cloud of disappointment fell over him.

He only gave up when he'd wasted more than a month on this futile search. On August 15th, seeing the empty streets on account of the holiday, he realized the time had come to accept reality and recognize chance can be cruel as well, snuffing out the flicker of hope with which we sometimes try to ignite our lives.

Before boarding the train, Diana dropped the last photo on the platform. She was the only one who noticed the piece of card lost on the cement, soon covered by the first footstep to dirty its initial shine. This footstep would be followed by others, since the train was about to leave and there were lots of people milling about the station. There remained her final portrait. Someone might notice it in a couple of hours, or several days later. Or perhaps no one would ever find it and it would be swept away with the other rubbish an employee collected the following day, to be packed together with other waste and burned in the local incinerator. Obviously she would have liked someone to find it, but she didn't mind the idea of it turning into a bit of ash and smoke. Whatever happened, her ritual was complete.

Since the lottery had been unusually generous to her and enabled her to abandon her routine job in an office, Diana had spent a large amount of time travelling, this had always been her greatest desire. She liked to travel alone, away from the tourist routes she'd gone on to begin with, which had taken her only to soulless, impersonal places. She would stay in the city she'd chosen for one or two weeks, soaking up the life going on in its squares and streets. She loved going to parties and concerts, watching people and talking to them, walking in areas that were busy and others that were more solitary. Always in search of the secret soul hidden in every city.

It was on her first trip to Florence that she decided to leave eight photographs of herself in different parts of every city she went to. One when she arrived, another on leaving, these two were obligatory. The rest she would drop in places where, for some reason, she'd felt the happiness of living with particular intensity. Looked at from the outside, this practice might seem a trifle ridiculous, she realized this. A kind of private performance whose sole author and solitary spectator she was, since she doubted the existence of a bored god watching her comings and goings from above. Leaving these photos was a way of prolonging her presence, so that something of hers would remain in places where she'd been happy: her face and name, the most personal, genuine thing she could offer the city that had been her home. Deep down, she realized there was nothing new in her behaviour, it was a modern version of times when visitors etched their name on the walls of monuments to show they had once been there. An absurd desire to immortalize ourselves we cannot avoid perhaps.

As the train pulled out of the station, Diana began to fantasize about the destination of the photos she'd left

A Photo in the Street

behind on this occasion. Eight images in a city flooded by light and Atlantic saltpetre. She liked to imagine someone would find one of the photos and play the game she so often indulged in: weaving stories on the basis of a face in some publication or glimpsed on some street. Perhaps there was someone right now imagining who this Diana could be, gazing at them from the abandoned photo. It was a useless fantasy, she knew this, but it didn't harm anybody. There was nothing to stop her dreaming of the lives of people who perhaps, at that same instant, were dreaming different lives for her, in a game of mirrors only chance or some god with time on his hands could control.

MEDITATION
BEFORE
THE FAMILY
PHOTO ALBUM

Time heals all. But what if time is the illness?

Wim Wenders, *Wings of Desire*

When I was a child, this country house was the centre of the universe. Summers back then were luminous and eternal, at least for us children lucky enough to come from wealthy families, and life was so full of surprises that each new day yielded a roller coaster of emotions. It's true we lived in Lugo for nine months of the year but, though it was longer, my memory of this time is uniform and grey, as grey as the city was in those years, confined between the stones of the wall and smothered by an overcast sky or the cold, damp mist that rose from the river and kept us company all winter.

I barely remember what kind of child I was in those early years, when my world was limited to home and the friars' college. I sometimes think life really began when I left the college and started at the boys' school; my brightest memories are of that period, the endless hours spent in the school's classrooms and corridors, the routine of doing homework in my room, the few hours' play in the square gardens, the visits with my mother to the cathedral… And the rain, the rain that fell incessantly, reinforcing the oppressive sensation that every day was an exact repetition of the day before. Time seemed to stagnate during the school year and didn't start up again until the first days of June, when the end of the exams heralded the beginning of the holidays and, with it, the start of our preparations to move to the paradise of our country home.

It must be true that space is as subjective as time because, looked at from the perspective of today, it's ridiculous the journey from Lugo to here struck me as an adventure, given that nowadays it takes less than half an hour to travel the twenty odd miles. Back then the miles separating the city from paradise were much longer and promised to be as exciting as the trips to exotic lands undertaken by the characters in Verne's novels, my staple diet in that period.

It was my father who brought us here in the family car, though he then went back to Lugo to attend to his notary's office, which only stopped working in August. If I close my eyes, I can still see the old black Hispano-Suiza full of boxes and suitcases. My mother occupied the other front seat while my sisters and I made do in the back with Rosa, the maid who looked after us at home throughout the year and kept us company in the summer months.

The country house is a couple of miles from Vilalba, in a place called Revolta. Despite the irremediable abandonment of these lands in recent years, they still retain a large part of the beauty they had before. Most of the chestnut groves and oak woods I played in are still standing, the encroachment of the eucalyptuses hasn't reached this far. But the fields aren't ploughed as they used to be, and crops of potatoes and wheat have been replaced by grassy meadows or, most often, by broom, gorse and ferns. The paths I walked along are now overgrown with brambles, which no one bothers to clear.

It may be difficult to understand from an adult's viewpoint, but the country house seemed enormous to me then, with all its corridors and rooms, some of them with the door always locked, rooms I imagined as brimming with mystery, like the secret chamber in Bluebeard's castle, which filled me with a diffuse fear. The garden and vegetable patch at the back were like a continent I could explore for days on end without ever growing bored.

We came here because this was where my maternal grandmother, Laura, lived with Aunt Carmiña, my mother's sister, who had remained single. My grandfather had died before I was two and the only image I had of him was that of the family photographs on display in the various rooms, portraits of ghosts since most of the people in them had long since passed away.

Grandma Laura was as fat as a barrel and always wore dark clothes, which made her look older than she was. She spent most of the time sitting in an armchair next to the balcony, directing the work of the maids. Aunt Carmiña also dressed in dark colours, but she wasn't like Grandma at all. She was tall and thin, and led a very independent life. She drove her own car, which was quite unusual back then, and went to Vilalba in it every day to manage a chemist's shop she looked after more out of pleasure than necessity, I suppose, to get away from a building that, now that I know more about life, I think may have represented a prison for her.

Apart from Mother and Aunt Carmiña, Grandma had two other children, who also came to spend the summer in the country with their families. At the end of June, like us, Aunt Elisa would turn up. She had lived in Ferrol since marrying Uncle Adolfo, a navy commander who seemed to have an aversion to smiling. She brought my four cousins, my partners in adventure, especially Violeta, who was a few months younger than me and the object of my attentions until well into my teens. Later, in August, my uncle and aunt from Madrid would arrive. Uncle Carlos occupied an important position in the Ministry of Industry, while Aunt María had a beauty that fascinated us children and seemed to observe everything around her with a cold, distant gaze, as if she were already counting the days until their return to Madrid in September. Their two children were about to leave the realm of childhood, but often took part in our games.

I think the country house was a paradise not just for me, but for all my cousins. We boys and girls formed a tribe which, though it lived in the same building as the adults, was governed by different rules and timetables. Rules that had nothing to do with those of our elders, who went about their lives as if we did not exist. It was the maids who took care of us, making sure we were properly fed and clothed. For the rest of the day, we were as free and happy-go-lucky as castaways left on a desert island.

All paradises run out eventually, though I didn't know this back then. Grandma Laura died in 1970, just after I turned twenty. Her children decided to sell all the many lands and properties and share out the money. The only thing that wasn't sold was the country house, where Aunt Carmiña carried on living until her death

MEDITATION BEFORE THE FAMILY PHOTO ALBUM

at Christmas three years ago. After my grandmother passed on, nothing was ever the same. It seems she was the thread that bound the four children together, since the distance between them dates from those years. Or perhaps it began much earlier, and all Grandma Laura's death did was mark the end of an era there was no point prolonging. The fact they lived in separate cities, their own children who'd grown up and had other interests… everything contributed to the decay of their relationship. The bonds between us cousins also loosened, each of us discovered life gets complicated and, despite our family's wealth, times were changing, we had to build a future based on our dreams.

I studied law in Santiago and then moved to Coruña. I married Berta and our two daughters were born. Life, at least from an economic point of view, was kind to me; better not to talk about other points of view, now is not the time to uncover the misfortunes we all have to endure. My father died in 1991, my mother a few months later. My uncles and aunts also passed on during this decade, as if there were some kind of tacit agreement between them to abandon this world before the end of the twentieth century. The last to leave was Aunt Carmiña, who still invited us to her country home each summer to celebrate the feast of St Raymond Nonnatus. She died in 1999 and left her inheritance to all nine nephews and nieces; a generous inheritance, it has to be said, the chemist's shop was profitable and she'd always led an austere life.

At a meeting to divide the inheritance, I proposed not selling the country house because I wanted to buy it. None of my cousins objected, so long as I paid them their share. My wife was not in favour of the idea, she thought it was tying up capital in an unproductive asset, but I received the unexpected support of Luz, my younger daughter, who seems to feel the same fascination for the house I did as a child.

Since the building was in a state of disrepair, I decided to carry out restoration work, especially on the northern side, where there were rooms that had never been used. I remember them being closed when I was little. The architect in charge of the project suggested pulling down some partition walls, since some of the rooms were tiny and there was no reason to keep them like this.

This autumn, having overcome numerous bureaucratic obstacles, we finally started work. In accordance with the new plans, the old inner walls were destroyed. In the carefully concealed gap between the walls of two of the rooms, the workmen discovered a whole skeleton in a magnificent state of preservation. It belonged to a young man in his twenties, and this particular chamber had been made to hold his corpse. It had been there for more than half a century, according to the coroner's report. This report explained the cause of his death in unnecessary detail: the perforated skull and bullet lying at the bottom were clear enough evidence for everyone to see.[1]

Since then, I haven't stopped gazing at this old family photo album and trying to work out, among all the stern faces, which is the one with a murderous look in its eyes.

---

[1] A similar discovery forms the basis of the author's novel *Corridors of Shadow* (2016).

AFTER ALL THESE YEARS

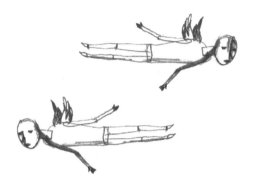

They say life is a shhhhhooting star
crossing the night sky.

Celso Emilio Ferreiro, *Where the World Is Called Celanova*

Yesterday Adrián died. Carme just rang to give me the news. She said she'd found out from the obituary in today's newspaper. She always reads them, the obituaries, scours them from top to bottom. "I imagined you'd want to know. Since you were asking about him just the other day... The funeral's today at seven, they're bringing him from Barcelona. You're still in time to come, if you want. You know you're welcome to stay the night in our house."

I thanked her and said no, I wouldn't go; there wasn't a coach and I didn't want to bother any of my children. I didn't tell her this, but the truth is I wouldn't have gone even if I had lived in Mondoñedo. Nor did I say anything about what I felt, they're intimate feelings I do not wish to share with anyone.

Carme may not have understood anyway. I'd have had to explain there are times death does not bring tears and sadness in its wake. Sometimes what it leaves are happy images stored in the memory like a forgotten treasure. What do I care whether Adrián died yesterday or the day before, if I removed him from my life many years ago? What really matters are the memories. They're all I have left, my hidden treasure, the only thing no one can take from me while I still have breath.

While I still have breath… I also feel the scythe of death moving closer, there comes a time when the strange thing is not to be thinking about it. I spoke to Iria, my eldest grandchild, about this a few weeks ago. It all began because she'd read in a book that people don't die outright so long as someone still remembers them, we all carry on living somehow in the minds of those who loved us. She liked the idea, I suppose it was her way of telling me how much she loved me. Now I think perhaps the person who wrote this was right, I'm unable to imagine Adrián as dead. In my mind, he's as alive as on the autumn night I first saw him.

I met Adrián at the feast of St Luke in Mondoñedo, 1964. I'd gone to spend a few days with my uncle and aunt, as I'd been doing ever since I was a child. My cousin Carme and I were the same age, we got on very well together, my parents were happy to let me go. As for me, used as I was to staying the whole year in Lanzós (except for the occasional trip to Vilalba or Lugo), the week I spent every autumn in Mondoñedo was a wonderful gift I looked forward to with great anticipation.

When I tell this to Iria, who is used to being taken everywhere by her parents, she always asks me why we didn't travel more often. She finds it difficult to understand what the world was like back then, and I don't blame her, I myself am surprised at times. From Lanzós to Vilalba is barely six miles! But at the time they seemed like different worlds, we only went to town on market days or in an emergency to see the doctor. So it's hardly strange I should be so keen to travel to Mondoñedo, even though the journey by coach took so long.

That autumn, I had an extra special reason for wanting to go. I needed to get away for a few days, so I could reflect on the direction my life was taking. I'd just turned twenty and had been engaged to Suso for several months. Suso came from Goiriz, I'd known him for years, he was related to the Louzaos and always visited their house during the feast of Our Lady of Mount Carmel. I'd exchanged words with him before, but when we got together was in January, at the feast of St Julian. We were out dancing all night and, when it was time to go, Suso offered to take me home on his motorbike. I turned him down, of course. A formal girl had no business accepting an offer like that. But since we liked each other's company, we agreed to meet on market day in Vilalba in February.

It was then he proposed going out together, after we'd spent a large part of the afternoon walking up and down the main street, waiting for the local cinema to open. They were showing a western I liked a lot, I still remember its name, *The Searchers*. Suso was very affectionate the whole time and, flattered by his attention, I ended up saying yes. After that, not a week went by when he didn't come and visit me at home on at least two occasions. Every Wednesday and Sunday, he would take his motorbike and make the journey from Goiriz to Lanzós, even when it was snowing or bucketing down. We would chat for a couple of hours in the yard outside, where we were visible from the kitchen. Or, if the weather was nice, we would walk down to the church and drink something in the bar there. When it was very cold, my mother would invite him inside and give him a cup of hot coffee before he left.

I liked the way he was always looking out for me, what's the use of denying it? And my parents were pleased as well. He was a formal boy and came from a good family, one of the richest in Goiriz. So, before I had time to consider whether or not I was doing the right thing, I found we were soon in a serious relationship and everyone considered us an item. Suso was five years older than me, had done his military service and was full of plans for the future. Though his family had plenty of lands, a farmer's life didn't attract him, he found it excessively harsh. He talked of moving to Ferrol like a relative of his. The shipyards needed people and paid well. He knew a fair bit about engineering, it was something he enjoyed.

Hearing him talk of these projects frightened me. Suso was convinced we'd get married and make our life in Ferrol. I felt dizzy whenever the topic came up in conversation. Everything was going too fast, I had the impression my life was running out of control. So I was particularly happy to go to Mondoñedo for a few days. I needed to get away and clear my head, understand why the idea of marriage scared me so much. I fancied having a good time with Carme and her friends, messing about for another year like the young girl I was.

The first time I saw Adrián was in the dance in the clearing. There was another dance further down, in the cathedral square, but Carme preferred the avenue of trees, she felt freer there. In the square, the balconies and windows were full of people who kept an eye on who was dancing with who and in what way, so that they could give a running commentary and criticize anyone who fell out of line. The clearing was also busy with old people whose only occupation was to watch couples dance, but the space was much bigger and there wasn't so much light.

I noticed Adrián as soon as I saw him, lest anyone should tell me there's no love at first sight. He was similarly smitten; whenever I looked, he had his eyes on me. Dances then were not like today, or so my granddaughters tell me. We girls danced in pairs and it was the boys who had to come and invite us, in pairs as well. So we always had the upper hand. If we didn't like them, we could say no and carry on dancing, waiting for boys we liked more to approach.

Adrián acted intelligently, he came to ask us to dance with Miguel, someone Carme had a crush on. I suppose they must have planned it beforehand, how else could it have been just the two of them? We could hardly say no, we both enjoyed their company, so I separated from Carme and joined him. They were playing "Two Gardenias" by Antonio Machín. If I close my eyes, I can still hear it. To begin with, he was quiet, as if his whole attention was focused on the lyrics, but he soon started talking, asking me the typical questions: what's your name, where are you from, what are you doing in Mondoñedo, what do you think of this year's celebrations… I gave him short, curt answers, as if obliged to do so, but inside I felt so nervous and joyful it was all I could do to keep him from noticing. I found it difficult to admit, I was engaged after all, but I was drawn to this pleasant man. My words could deny it, but my body didn't stop shouting it out loud for as long as the dance lasted.

We separated at the end of the song, as was the custom, and I went back to Carme. My cousin was all aflutter, as if something extraordinary had taken place in the few minutes we'd been apart. She wanted to know if I would mind dancing with them for the rest of the evening. Miguel had asked while they were dancing, but she hadn't wanted to give an answer until she knew my opinion. I said I didn't mind, I liked my partner as well, so when they came to take us a little later, we ended up dancing with them the whole night, until it was time to return home.

We did the same the next three nights, for as long as there was dancing. Everything I knew about Adrián I found out then. He worked in his father's carpentry workshop in Vilanova de Lourenzá. He loved listening to music and was skilled at playing the guitar. He had a record player, something unusual at the time, and kept talking of singers he knew about thanks to the records a relative of his brought back from Paris. He also loved to read and confessed he spent a large part of his earnings on books. When he asked me if I liked reading as well, I said I did, even though it wasn't true. It was good I lied because this encouraged him to talk about his books. He could retell the stories he'd read extremely well, it was a pleasure listening to him.

I was in seventh heaven, rarely had I felt so happy. I was far away from home, had nothing to do, was intent on having a good time, counting the hours until evening. They were four very special nights, one of those experiences that lets you glimpse something better behind the ordinary routine of every day.

I returned to Lanzós with more pain than any other year, resigned to letting the passing of the weeks smother the pretty dream that had begun to take shape during my stay in Mondoñedo. But this didn't happen, because a few days later I received a parcel at home. It was the first I'd ever been sent; back then, it was an event to receive a letter, let alone a parcel. And it had my name on it, Elvira Campos Graña, that much was clear. My surprise turned to emotion when I saw the sender's name, since it had been posted by Adrián. I had to disguise my feelings because Miguel, the local postman, arrived when we were all having lunch in the kitchen. Fortunately he sat down to drink some coffee, as was his custom, and I stole upstairs to my room, where I could open the parcel.

Inside, carefully wrapped, was a book with dark crimson covers. It's the same I have now before me: *Rhymes and Legends* by Gustavo Adolfo Bécquer, number three in the Austral series. Inside the pages of the book was a long letter from Adrián and a photo of him taken in Mondoñedo, sitting on the steps opposite the cathedral.

The letter was three pages long and I read it through several times, as if I needed to do so to understand fully what Adrián was saying. He'd got my address from Carme and sent the book because he was sure I would like Bécquer's poetry. He told me things about his life, talked of records and books, remembered our conversations the evenings we'd spent together during the feast of St Luke. And he asked when I'd be coming back to Mondoñedo. He wanted to see me again, said he couldn't stop thinking about me. At the end, he asked me to reply and send a photo of me.

I wrote to him a few days later, using the brief moments I was alone in the house, because I didn't want anyone to know. I waited until there was a market day in Vilalba to post the letter in the post office; in Lanzós, I'd have had to leave it in the shop where the post was collected and everybody would have found out. Mine was a shorter letter, there was no way I was going to say how much I'd enjoyed his company, but I enclosed a studio portrait taken that summer in Vilalba by the photographer who works near the church, above Severino's hair salon. I looked very pretty, wearing the print dress my uncle had brought from Coruña, no one ever took a photo like that of me again.

I received Adrián's second letter shortly afterwards. He must have spoken to Carme about me, because he hinted he knew I had a boyfriend, though he never mentioned him by name. He went on to insist how much he liked me, though we'd only known each other for a few nights, and couldn't stop thinking about me. It was a lovely letter, it was obvious how many books he'd read, he used words that were like caresses. Towards the end, he declared I was the woman of his life and he'd do anything to see me again. He used those very words and they sent my heart into a spin.

This letter was followed by other longer, more passionate missives, despite the brevity of my replies. When I received the fifth letter, I decided not to write back. I was aware I was getting into a situation I couldn't handle. Suso carried on visiting me, as was his habit; he entered the house now, my parents were delighted with him. He talked more and more about getting married, moving to Ferrol and settling there.

He was convinced working the land was for fools and he didn't want to waste his life like this. He dreamed of boats, the sea, of living in a city, where life was easier and offered everything.

I liked Suso, he was a good boy and hard-working. But when I secretly read those emotional love poems in the book by Bécquer, I thought of Adrián. During the day, despite all the housework I had to do, I would find myself staring into space, holding the broom or making the beds, with thoughts of Adrián and the music of some of the songs we'd danced together going round inside my head. I was trapped in the midst of a doubt that accompanied me everywhere and I didn't know what to do. At home, they must have noticed my confusion, but ignored its cause; Suso must have noticed as well, though he never said anything.

One day, I decided to reveal all my doubts to my mother, I had to talk to someone I could trust if I didn't want this dejection to consume me. But she barely let me speak, her expression changed as soon as she understood what it was I was trying to tell her. She was furious, shouting as if there had been a tragedy. I was very sorry I'd opened my mouth! Only I could think, having such a lovely boyfriend, to lose my head over someone who had plied me with sweet words. If I left Suso, there would be a scandal in the whole parish, no water would wash me clean. We would be on everyone's lips for years and I could forget any other boy having formal intentions towards me.

I let myself be convinced. This was another time and I didn't know any better. Suso represented security, he was at my side and loved me. Adrián was nothing but an image, a wily seducer who lived far away and hadn't even bothered to travel the distance to Lanzós. He was probably just playing with me, the pretty things he said were no doubt copied out of the books he read. I sent him a short letter, asking him not to write anymore, I was formally engaged and his words were just confusing me. If he wrote any more letters, they never reached me; my mother could easily have hidden them from me, if that was what she wanted.

Suso and I were married in 1966. He had left for Ferrol a few months earlier and soon got a job at Astano, I already said he was a gifted engineer. His family helped him buy a flat in San Valentín, a new part of Fene that had been built near the docks. After we were married, I went to join him in Fene. We both missed the contact with the land, but soon grew used to our new life. It was then they opened Pías Bridge, which brought Ferrol that much closer; every Sunday, we went for a walk there, it was always full of people.

Suso liked his work, for years he felt proud of what he was doing. Astano started building those huge oil tankers, it was impressive watching them grow day by day in the docks. From the windows of the flat, I could see the dark hulk of the boat, the sparks of the welders, and hear the intense murmur of men working on it. Even I was proud whenever one was launched and people came down to see the ceremony. The biggest of them all was the *Arteaga* in May 1972. A 385,000-ton ship! Fene that day was bustling; I shall never forget my husband's face when that huge thing rolled down the slipway and landed gently in the water.

After All These Years

Suso worked long hours and was paid well, we had everything we needed at home: a washing machine, TV, fridge... They were years of plenty and, at the time, we thought they would last forever. Our three children were born in the flat and we stayed there until we moved to this house in Perlío, shortly after Franco's death. A big, new house with a quarter acre of land, one of the best in the region. Life treated us well, it would be wrong of me to complain. We had our problems – what marriage doesn't? – but we raised our children and got ahead. And, needless to say, I forgot all about my youthful romance. I worked so hard to put it out of my head I ended up consigning it to a forgotten corner of my memory.

When things got worse was in 1984, with the naval reorganization brought in by the Socialists. They said it was the price we had to pay if we wanted to enter Europe. This is something I never understood, either then or now, but the fact is from one day to the next Astano no longer had ships to build and half the workforce wasn't needed. With all the richness there had been in Ferrol! Bad times came and people started to be without work. A real shame, there were lots who had to leave. Some of our neighbours went to the Canaries, others returned to the village they'd left years before. We weren't the worst hit, at the time of the crisis we had a house of our own and some savings, Suso had always been careful. We had to tighten our belts, of course, our younger children were still studying; but Celia, the eldest, had got a job in the local town hall and would soon be married.

The thing my husband couldn't stomach was becoming unemployed. He managed to escape the initial effects of the naval reorganization, but it ended up affecting him as well. He lost his job in 1988, at the age of forty-nine. Having nothing to do all day was what most depressed him. His character changed, he grew bitter. He stayed away from home, said it was too small for him. I encouraged him to work outside, in the garden, he had always enjoyed relaxing there. The idea was to keep him busy, but it was impossible. To make matters worse, he didn't take care of himself. All that smoking, always with a cigarette in his mouth, anyone could see it wasn't good. When he suffered a second heart attack in 1997, he couldn't get over it. He died aged fifty-seven, poor thing, he was still very young. And I was a widow at the age of fifty-two, I'd never imagined this happening to me. I'm just glad my three children were around, they're the ones who helped me get through such a difficult situation.

My mother died three years later, my father had died long before, and I inherited the house in Lanzós. When the inheritance was divided up, at the insistence of my children, who'd always loved going there, I opted to receive less than my brother and sister in exchange for keeping the house. They didn't mind, they'd both built properties of their own and had no need to set about repairing a house that was already so old.

Last summer, rummaging in the attic, Iria found a wooden box with my name written on the outside. Had someone asked me about it, I'd have said I didn't know what they were talking about, I'd completely forgotten about it. That's how our brain works, it remembers only what it chooses. But when she brought it down and showed it to me, of course I remembered at once. A week before marrying, I'd used this box to store all the objects I had in drawers in my room so that no one else would meddle with them. My idea was to take the box to Ferrol at a later date, but I never did. How could I have forgotten it for so long?

As soon as I opened it, the first thing that caught my eye was a large buff envelope. Inside I found the book by Bécquer along with Adrián's letters and photo. Suddenly a part of my life I'd thought was behind me came flooding back. These belongings aroused feelings I didn't know I still had: unease, anxiety, pain, emptiness. It was a surprise attack and, to begin with, I felt that life was being unfair to me. Now that I'd chosen my road, a memory appeared to show me there was another life I could have led.

Over the next few days, I made enquiries through Carme. She'd carried on living in Mondoñedo, Vilanova is a step away, distances aren't what they used to be. It can't have been all that difficult to obtain the information, everybody knows each other in small towns. So it was I found out Adrián had left for Barcelona many years earlier, around the same time we'd moved to Fene. He'd married there, but the relationship can't have gone well and he'd ended up separating. He would come back to Vilanova in the holidays, he still had two sisters living there.

Memory is treacherous, it comes and goes at will, plays with us in a way we are powerless to prevent. Imagination is more loyal, we can direct it. And so, ever since recovering the box, I like to imagine that Adrián held onto my photo, stole a glance at it from day to day, my smile kept him company all that time we lived apart. Whether or not it was like this, I neither know nor care. What does it matter after all these years!

I've heard during the final moments of our lives the images of everything that's happened to us pass rapidly in front of our eyes, like a film being projected at high speed. I don't know if this is true, God keep me from finding out for many years. But my promise here today, having learned of Adrián's death, is to carry his photo always with me, to look at it again and again in the time I have left, even though I am forced to conceal it from my children.

That way, when death comes along and that crazy film is projected before my eyes, I may just manage to anchor my memory to the face of Adrián, that boy who gave me the first book that was truly mine, the man with whom destiny may have wanted to offer me the chance to lead a happier life.

A River of Words

He who gives a word gives a gift.

José Ángel Valente, *The Innocent*

To begin with, I wasn't at all sure it was a good idea. It came to me as I was contemplating those pieces of paper with all kinds of adverts people stick up in busy places. Anyone who lives in a city knows them well, though to read their content you have to go up close, they're almost always in small type: "Lady available to babysit on a hourly basis," "We'll take your dog for a walk," "24-hour locksmiths," "Maths graduate offers private lessons"… They're easy to spot, the page has been cut at the bottom, with strips showing the phone number you have to ring. I thought nobody paid them any attention, but I changed my mind when I began to notice how almost all the tickets would disappear in a couple of hours.

So it's hardly surprising I should think up this idea, having come across another of those books that gladdens the heart and makes you want to live. Having read it, I was seized by the desire I always feel in such cases: to phone my friends, to shout in the middle of the street, to let the whole world know. To inform people they shouldn't carry on living without reading this book, it contains too much beauty simply to ignore.

The idea came to me spontaneously. I had barely thought it out when I was in front of the computer, copying the opening lines from a book of short stories that had absorbed me over the preceding days. I did it in 21-point type with generous spacing, there was no way I wanted it to get lost among all the other advertisements:

I dream of the first cherry of summer. I give it to her and she puts it in her mouth, looks at me with warm, sinful eyes, as she possesses the flesh. Suddenly, she kisses me and gives it back to me with her tongue. And I'm hers forever, the cherry stone rolling up and down the keyboard of my teeth all day long like a wild, musical note.

I printed twenty copies on blue paper. I then had to cut the strips at the bottom; it was tedious work, but worth the effort. On them, instead of a phone number, I wrote the title of the book and the name of its author. If someone wanted to know more about the story hidden behind these lines, they would find there the clue that would permit them to enter the story and unearth its wonders.

I stuck the sheets up all over my neighbourhood. Feeling a little ashamed, I got up early and posted them while it was still dark, on the way to work. Coming back from the office, the first thing I did was check the places where I'd left the sheets. My heart filled with optimism as I saw most of the strips had been taken. It was much more than I'd expected, a clear sign my messages were now in the hands of strangers.

Encouraged by my success, I decided to have another go. This time I chose the opening lines from one of those books I regularly reread, wishing to experience again the intense emotion I felt on the first occasion:

It was the summer that men first walked on the moon. I was very young back then, but I did not believe there would ever be a future. I wanted to live dangerously, to push myself as far as I could go, and then see what happened to me when I got there. As it turned out, I nearly did not make it. Little by little, I saw my money dwindle to zero; I lost my apartment; I wound up living in the streets. If not for a girl named Kitty Wu, I probably would have starved to death.

I quickly discovered the tickets at the bottom disappeared soon after I left them. The system worked! I carried on putting up new texts every three or four days, since I wanted to allow enough time for each one to have the desired effect. On reaching the tenth sheet, I decided to do something special. I bought some higher quality paper and, after lots of doubts, selected the opening to a book that had had a strong influence on me the year long before when I first read it:

As Gregor Samsa awoke one morning from uneasy dreams he found himself transformed in his bed into a gigantic insect. He was lying on his hard, as it were armour-plated, back and when he lifted his head a little he could see his domelike brown belly divided into stiff arched segments on top of which the bed quilt could hardly keep in position and was about to

slide off completely. His numerous legs, which were pitifully thin compared to the rest of his bulk, waved helplessly before his eyes.

The following morning, when I went outside to stick up the posters, I was amazed to see someone else had already posted some sheets. I felt an overwhelming emotion, which grew when I realized this anonymous person had dared to leave some poetry, thereby showing up all those who wrongly claim poetry as a minority genre:

Your hair is a rick,
your eyes are fields, your eyes
are green as oak leaves
and green as ferns;
your breasts are like kids grazing
outside the city and your hands
are swallows.
Your heart
is a beach
at that hour of the gloaming when everybody leaves
the sand warm,
your embrace has the shape of a wren's nest,
your heat has nothing to do with winter.

I didn't just tear off a ticket. Having posted my sheets as well, I kept an eye out all day to see how this new suggestion would be received. The reception it got was extraordinary, the tickets disappeared even more quickly. I was over the moon! I now knew there was someone nearby who was also prepared to share the emotion

147

they had felt on reading one of those books that lights up your life.

But my greatest surprise came the following Monday. When I got up to leave some sheets with a new text, I found entire streets covered in pieces of coloured paper: they were on street corners, on lamp-posts, on the doors of shops, on traffic lights, on bus stops… The whole of my neighbourhood was brimming with wonderful texts and tickets hanging temptingly underneath them, like the ripe fruit of exotic trees.

I can't say if this miracle will last forever or be just an autumnal passion that will disappear with the arrival of the rain. But something tells me it's not a mere flash in the pan, there are things, like a snowball rolling down the hillside, that only need an initial push to start growing. Who knows! This epidemic may spread to engulf the whole city, thousands of people may decide to fill the streets with rivers of words. And among them, my heart tells me, will be the woman I'm waiting for, the unknown love with whom I hope to share each and every day of my existence.

Of LOVE and BOOKS

This book took shape slowly over several years, almost subterraneously, since it took me some time to realize that, though they were written at different stages, the stories in it have a common thread that gives unity to the whole. They all talk of the importance of love, that feeling that can transform us more deeply than any other, and also of its absence, the void it leaves in people when the twists and turns of life make it impossible. Some of these stories were previously published in magazines or collective books, always in earlier versions. They were all rewritten and extended for the purposes of this volume and I consider them now to be entirely original.

The list of people to whom I owe my thanks is very long and I shall mention only a few of them here. There are stories here that would not exist had someone not asked me to write them or given me the idea for them. Isabel Soto and Antonio Ventura, for different reasons, are responsible for the existence of "A Radiant Silence." The same is true of Santiago Jaureguizar and "August Love," of which he published a much shorter version in *El Progreso*. "A Ghost Story" arose from a request by Xosé Neira Cruz, as did "Rivers of Memory" from a request by Ana Romaní and Paulino Novo. Meanwhile, Manuel Bragado and Xavier Senín had a lot to do with the creation of some of these stories.

Nothing Really Matters in Life More Than Love is also, in its own way, a book about the importance of reading in our lives, containing as it does an open tribute to other books I'm especially fond of, from which I include short excerpts. I would be delighted to point readers in the direction of the books these extracts are taken from. Here are the main references:

Most of them are in "A Radiant Silence." "Rapunzel" is an unforgettable folk-tale and there are several versions, the best known perhaps being that of the Brothers Grimm. "Be My Limit," the poem on the first card Sara finds, is by José Ángel Valente and belongs to his book *Memory and Signs*, included in the Spanish anthology of his work *Punto cero* (*Point Zero*), first published in 1972 and later reissued in 1980. The translation of Valente's poem is by Thomas Christensen from the anthology in English *Landscape with Yellow Birds*. "Barcarole," the poem by Pablo Neruda she finds on the second card, is in *Residence on Earth*, one of the Chilean author's most fascinating books, and included in his *Selected Poems*, edited and translated by Nathaniel Tarn. The verses from the third card come from the end of an extraordinary poem by Yeats, "Aedh Wishes for the Cloths of Heaven," in *The Wind among the Reeds*. The verses from the poems Pablo the bookseller burns belong, in this order, to Xesús Manuel Valcárcel, José Ángel Valente, Pablo Neruda, Paul Éluard and Neruda again. The poem by Valcárcel is "Your Voice Is Like Wine" from the book *Door of Fire*. The poem by Valente is "Latitude" from the book *Mandorla*, translated by Thomas Christensen. The two poems by Neruda are "Leaning into the Afternoons" and "Every Day You Play" from the book *Twenty Love Poems and a Song of Despair*, again in his *Selected Poems*, this time translated by W. S. Merwin. The poem by Éluard is "The Curve of Your Eyes," translated by A. S. Kline and available online. The passage at the end of the story from *Oracle Night* by Paul Auster is abridged.

The verses quoted in the final sequence of "This Strange Lucidity" belong to a magnificent poem by Xulio López Valcárcel, "Another Poem of Gifts," included in his book *August Memory*.

The two poems by José Ángel Valente in "A Ghost Story" are "If after Death We Rise" and "Love Is in What We Put Forward" from the books *Fragments from a Future Book* and *Brief Sound* respectively, translated by Thomas Christensen in the anthology *Landscape with Yellow Birds*.

Finally, the texts in "A River of Words" belong, in this order, to the books *Vermeer's Milkmaid and Other Stories* by Manuel Rivas; *Moon Palace* by Paul Auster; *Metamorphosis* by Franz Kafka (translated by Willa and Edwin Muir); and *Door of Fire* by Xesús Manuel Valcárcel. Unless otherwise mentioned, English translations of texts are by Jonathan Dunne.

At the beginning of September 2007, when I was revising the texts in this book for the last time, Pablo Auladell finished his illustrations and posted a sample of what he'd done on his blog (http://pabloauladell.blogspot. com/). I already knew he was working on this project and every day in August I accessed his blog, which had been inactive since the beginning of July, eager to see the results. Finally, on the evening of September 5th, the miracle happened: there they were, on the screen, four illustrations from the book. They were amazing! I admire Pablo's work (I consider *La Tour Blanche*, for example, an essential album), but what met my eyes exceeded all my expectations. The four illustrations were of a stunning formal beauty and possessed, above all, intense emotion, much greater than that contained in my stories. So much so, I felt like writing a new story based on what each of them suggested to me, stories that could lead to other images, and new stories, in an unending game of mirrors. I am honoured that this book should be enriched by Pablo's illustrations, so full of life and impossible to forget.

Agustín Fernández Paz is a modern classic of Galician literature. His works often reflect on the lost world of childhood, the sheer expanse of new experiences. They sometimes involve characters whose road is blocked by their social condition, or supernatural elements that transport us into the realm of horror and suspense. Three novels have so far appeared in English: *Black Air* (2014), *Winter Letters* (2015) and *Corridors of Shadow* (2016).

Pablo Auladell is a highly successful illustrator from Alicante. He won the 2016 Spanish National Comic Award for his graphic novel based on Milton's *Paradise Lost*, published by Random House. Other well-known works include the album *La Tour Blanche*, published by Actes Sud in France. He teaches on the Masters in Illustration at Macerata in Italy.

For an up-to-date list of our publications, please visit www.smallstations.com